I0638768

Wanted: Dead Men

KENDELL FOSTER CROSSEN
Writing as
M.E. CHABER

STEEGER BOOKS / **2020**

PUBLISHED BY STEEGER BOOKS
Visit steegerbooks.com for more books like this.

PUBLISHING HISTORY

Hardcover
New York: Holt, Rinehart & Winston (A Rinehart Suspense Novel), November 1965. Dust jacket by Ben Feder, Inc.
Toronto: Holt, Rinehart & Winston of Canada, November 1965.
London: T. V. Boardman (American Bloodhound Mystery #528), 1966.

Paperback
New York: Paperback Library (63-460), A Milo March Mystery, #14, November 1970. Cover by Robert McGinnis.

ISBN: 978-1-61827-535-6

For Lisa

And I will make thee beds of roses and a thousand fragrant posies.

—Christopher Marlowe

CONTENTS

ONE

Milo March, Insurance Investigator—that's what it said on the door of my office on Madison Avenue in New York City. That's what it also said on the rent bill I'd just received. I looked in my checkbook. I had the rent all right, but not much over it. The rest of the mail was advertising pieces. So I picked up the *New York Times* and tried to forget the whole thing. It was going to be one of those days.

The phone rang. I picked up the receiver and said hello.

"Milo, my boy, how are you?" a masculine voice asked. It belonged to Martin Raymond, a vice-president for Intercontinental Insurance. Maybe it wasn't going to be a lost day after all. I do most of my work for Intercontinental.

"I was fine until the phone rang," I said. "Then I got a sudden attack of vice-presidentitis."

He chuckled. "That's my boy, always making with the fun lines. Got a minute?"

"Wait until I look at my watch," I said. "Yes, I think I have a minute."

"How about running over here? I think we have a small job for you."

"Is it all right if I stroll? I'm getting too old for running. But I'll be there as soon as I can reach my cane." I hung up.

Good old Martin Raymond. I was going to be back in the

money again. I took a final, loving drink from the bottle of brandy in my desk drawer, called my phone-answering service and told them I'd be in touch, and then took off. It was a short walk up Madison Avenue to the Intercontinental building, a neat little skyscraper of stone and glass looking as if it had been constructed so that people who lived in glass buildings could throw their own sculptured stones.

I stepped out of the elevator on the executive floor and stopped to appreciate the scenery—a redheaded receptionist who looked as if she'd taken a deep breath and held it.

"Hello, Mr. March," she said.

"Hold it, honey," I said. "Don't say another word. I want to remember you just as you are."

"Oh, you," she said, which was her idea of a witty remark. But then she didn't have to be witty. "Did you want to see Mr. Raymond?"

"No," I said truthfully, "but he wants to see me."

"His secretary said for you to come on back as soon as you arrived."

"He doesn't like me to stay out here and dally with the hired help," I said. "It just proves that he's going to grow up to be a dirty old man. See you later."

I went through the door on the left and down the corridor to Raymond's office. His secretary nodded for me to go in, and I entered the inner sanctum.

Martin Raymond has a passion for antique furniture, a fact which is impressed on anyone entering his office. Only none of it looks quite like it did in the early days of America. Just as two examples, there is a cobbler's bench which now supports ashtrays and an old cuckoo clock with a wooden bird that pops out on the hour and says "Intercontinental." Then there is an Early American sideboard which has been converted into a bar. Some Puritan cabinetmaker must be spinning in his grave.

"Milo, boy," he said, as I came in, "how are you? Help yourself to a drink. You know where the bar is."

I knew where the bar was, but it was so seldom that he suggested that I help myself, I knew it must be a case that had him nervous. Still, I'm not one to pass up an opportunity, so I went over and poured myself a brandy. I went back to the chair in front of his desk and lifted the glass.

"To higher premiums and fewer cases," I said solemnly.

"Still the jokes," he said with a laugh, but his heart wasn't in it. He swiveled his chair so he could look out the window in the direction of the East River. There wasn't anything to see there except a few garbage scows, but he ignored that. "We have a bit of a problem, Milo."

"No," I said in mock astonishment. "Not Intercontinental with its billions of dollars and a folder full of competent vice-presidents!"

He gave me a fleeting, pained look. "This is not a time for levity," he said. "Do you know anything about industrial spying?"

"Sure," I said promptly. "It's known as business ethics. If your competitor builds a better mousetrap, you hire someone to steal it before the world beats a path to his door. In the meantime, you hire other thugs to keep them from stealing your version of the mousetrap."

"Brutally put," he said, "but more or less accurate. For some time, we have been issuing policies insuring companies against such thefts. It goes along with the policies on their executives, theft, and so forth. It's a fairly lucrative business, but somewhat risky."

"And you've finally been nipped?"

He ignored the question, staring out at the garbage scows. "There are three very large companies concerned in the case at hand. Santee Chemical Corporation, Crossen Plastics, Inc., and the Palmieri-Foster Research Corporation. All three companies have offices here in New York; the first two have factories in Pennsylvania, and the third has a factory in Connecticut."

"It hardly sounds like the beginning of a serial by Mickey Spillane, but I'll go along to the next installment."

"In the last year," he continued, "Santee developed a new cleansing formula and a new deodorant, both of which were stolen and are now being manufactured in Europe. Crossen Plastics had developed, at great cost, a plastic that could be used in construction and which was at least as strong as steel, and another plastic, produced very cheaply, which could resist any degree of heat. These, too, were stolen and are now being produced in Europe." He stopped and lit a cigarette.

"And the third company?" I asked gently.

"We'll come to that in a minute," he said grimly. "There were also some employees involved. Robert Halsey and Dan Frame worked as chemists for Santee and both were involved with the new products. They both committed suicide just before it was discovered that their work had been stolen."

"Joint suicide?"

"No. Two weeks apart."

"And I suppose they were also insured?"

"Oh, yes," he said bitterly. "Two hundred thousand on each."

"Suicide clause?"

He made a face. "We waived it. They worked under extreme pressure, so ordinary policies didn't apply."

"And the premiums were higher?"

"Yes," he admitted reluctantly.

"Go ahead," I said.

"There were also two men who were important in developing the advances in plastics. Richard Matson and Carl Kelly. Good men. Shortly before those two inventions showed up in Europe, Matson was killed in a hit-and-run accident. A week later Kelly was the victim of a hit-and-run driver."

I was beginning to get the picture. "Both had insurance policies?"

"Yes."

"How much?"

"Two hundred thousand each."

"Double indemnity?"

"Yes." It was like a mournful cry in the streets.

"All right," I said. "What about the third company?"

"No one died there," he said. He was grabbing at straws.

"Well, that's a certain amount of progress. What did happen?"

"I can't tell you," he said glumly.

"Is that my job?" I asked. "To start guessing what the job is? This is a new type of insurance investigation."

"Maybe," he said. "I don't like it any better than you do. Milo, we have about three million dollars at stake. We can't save all of it. A large part will have to be paid, no matter what you turn up. But your work may help to stop further cases like this."

"And the third situation?" I asked.

"There is someone waiting to discuss it with you in our conference room. It's classified. I'm afraid that I know nothing about it except that we insured it."

"You mean you've given me the whole case?"

He sighed. "Pretty much, Milo. I can tell you that the four men I mentioned all answered help wanted advertisements between two or three months before the secrets were stolen. We don't know what the ads were, where they appeared, or who placed them. But we did learn that much from their wives. Apparently the ads were such that the men thought they might get much better jobs than they had. There must be some connection."

"Possibly," I said. "That's all?"

"That's all. I know it's a tough assignment, Milo. If you can solve it, we'll give you a good bonus in addition to your regular fees."

"Uh-uh," I said.

"What?"

"Uh-uh. I'm not sure it's a proper word, but it is in common usage. It means no."

"No what?"

"Maybe you haven't heard," I said, "but the cost of living is going up year by year. I haven't raised my prices in a long time. From now on, it's one hundred and fifty dollars a day and expenses."

"All right," he said, giving in so easily it surprised me. "You'll probably have to go to Europe on this case, so we'll give you five thousand advance expense money. If you need more, let us know."

Then I knew it was a serious case. Martin Raymond parted with a dollar as easily as he'd give up a lung.

"No file on the cases?" I asked.

"There's a file and it contains exactly what I've told you, but you can have it. My secretary will give it to you with the expense money and then take you to the conference room. I know you'll do a good job, Milo."

This certainly wasn't the Martin Raymond I knew, but then I guess we all crack up once in a while. I nodded gravely and left the office without saying anything more. The secretary handed me a manila folder and a fat white envelope. I peeked inside, and it was stuffed with hundred-dollar bills.

"You hit the jackpot this time, buster," she said. "Come along."

"Why not?" I muttered. "I've already seen everything."

I was wrong. I followed her down the corridor and she finally opened a door and motioned me inside. I entered and then stopped when I saw him sitting alone at the conference table.

His name was Sam Roberts and I'd known him for a long, long time. When I first knew him he was a colonel in the Army. Now he was a three-star general attached to the CIA, and every once in a while he would yank me out of the

Reserves into active duty so I could pull some chestnuts out of the fire for him.

"Oh, no!" I said.

"Hello, Milo," he said mildly—too mildly.

"I won't do it," I said. "Whatever it is. I'll appeal to my Congressman. It's a free country and I'm not going back into the Army—even for you."

"Who asked you to?" he said.

"And I'm not going to volunteer for the CIA," I said flatly.

"Civilian life is softening you up," he said sadly. "I didn't hear any mention of such an organization."

"Then what are you doing here?"

"You taking the job for Intercontinental?" he countered.

"Yes."

"Then I'm here to tell you about the third plant."

"The Palmieri-Foster Research Corporation?"

"The same," he said.

"Something is missing from their company, too?"

"Something is missing, all right," he said grimly. "Two somethings."

"What?"

"I can't give you complete details," he said. "You have a very high security rating, Milo, but everything that Palmieri-Foster does is about as top secret as it's possible to get. All I can tell you is that they have developed an electronic device about the size of a walnut that will make a missile or a rocket do everything except play tennis, and I'm not sure it couldn't do that. I can't emphasize how important it is."

"It's missing," I guessed.

"One model is. So is the man who invented it—Angus Watson."

"You think he went over to the other side?"

"I'd gamble my life he didn't. At least, not voluntarily."

I made another guess. "He answered an ad?"

He nodded. "But at our request. We are well aware of the industrial espionage which goes on, but most of the time it has nothing to do with us. We do, however, check all such ads automatically, especially when it seems an infringement on products related to national security. Palmieri-Foster Research is located in a small town in Connecticut. About six weeks ago an ad appeared in the local paper to set up interviews with electronic engineers. It sounded as if it were aimed at that one particular company. Those ads are fishing expeditions, so we sent the biggest fish in the company, thinking he would spot anything that was wrong."

"And?"

"That was the last time Angus Watson was seen. He never returned to his home or office, and there is no record that he was ever seen again after entering the Concord Hotel where the interview was to be held."

"He wasn't covered?"

"Oh, yes, he was covered. Three of our best men. He entered the hotel and vanished."

"Maybe he vanished voluntarily?"

"No," he said strongly. "We're positive that he didn't."

"Okay," I said. "I think you mentioned that a model of his invention also disappeared?"

"Yes."

"And I suppose," I said dryly, "that you also suggested that Angus Watson take along a model of this valuable and secret invention in order to make his interview more realistic?"

He looked embarrassed, an unusual expression for General Roberts. "I'd better explain something about Watson ..."

"It might help," I said gently.

"Angus Watson is—or was—one of the most valuable men we had in electronics. He was something of a genius. This was not the first breakthrough he accomplished for us. He also had peculiar methods of operating and quite often did his most important work in his own home in the middle of the night. For several years he has been permitted to take work home with him. I think you are aware of how unusual this is."

" 'Unusual' is a kind word."

"I know, I know," he said with irritation. "It took a special order to give him permission to take work home. He was probably checked more often than any individual in the country, and was completely cleared every time. I am personally convinced that these clearances were all correct."

"All right," I said. I was familiar with Intercontinental conference rooms, so I went over and slid back a panel door in the wall to reveal a well-equipped bar. I made myself a drink and walked back to the table. "So he had a model of the invention in his home and in some way he managed to leave the hotel, go to his home, and get it without your three men seeing him."

He shook his head. "That is impossible. We also had men watching his house. In fact, we've had men stationed there for months, and he never went near his home the day he vanished. Nor did anyone else."

"I suppose there is another explanation?"

He was still embarrassed and I soon found out the reason. "There is one thing we didn't know," he admitted. "I told you this electronic device was about the size of a walnut. Watson apparently felt that he could still make improvements in it, and he was in the habit of carrying the model in his pocket. He liked to take long walks when he was working on a problem, and he carried the model with him."

"Including to the interview?"

"Yes," he said gloomily. "The Old Man is raising hell."

"I wonder why?" I murmured. "General, you have a lot of bright young bloodhounds working for you. They must have turned up something—at least one little clue."

He shook his head. "I'm afraid not. The advertisement was placed by a man who gave the name of C. Jackson. He rented three adjoining rooms in the Concord Hotel for the purpose of holding interviews. When he registered, he gave his home address, which turned out to be false. The description of him we got from various people in Connecticut is very superficial. He is about five feet eight, on the heavy side, dark hair parted on the left side, ruddy complexion. That's about it. It could fit several thousand people."

"You went over the rooms?"

"Yes. There were no prints in the rooms. Everything had been wiped clean. Not even any evidence that anyone had been there. We vacuumed the rooms, naturally, and we have a few samples of dark hair, a small amount of dandruff, and some cigarette ashes—and a few small tufts from a brown suit which was probably made in England. That's it."

"Was Watson the only man interviewed?"

"No. Four men were interviewed before Watson arrived. Their interviews were very short, and they had the distinct impression that Mr. Jackson was not interested in them. Watson was the fifth—and last—one to enter the suite."

"No one saw him leave?"

"No."

"What about this Jackson? Anyone see him leave?"

"No."

"Did he have much luggage?"

"One small suitcase."

"Car?"

"No. He arrived in a taxi when he checked in."

"I presume you looked into possible means of leaving the town?"

"Of course. Results were negative."

"The same thing applies to Watson?"

"Yes. He was not seen after entering the suite."

"What else have you done, General?"

"We had an artist draw a portrait of the man from the descriptions we received, and we had copies run off. We have also circulated copies of a photograph of Watson."

"No results?"

He shook his head. "Nothing so far."

"What are you doing here?" I asked bluntly.

"We knew that Intercontinental carried a policy on Watson and also had written the insurance for the plant. At first, we intended to ask them to stay out of this case because of the security angle. Then we learned they were planning on assigning you to all three cases, so we made contact with them and offered to brief you to the extent that is possible. If someone has to be messing around in the case, we'd rather it was you."

"Am I supposed to be grateful?"

He started to get angry but then realized that I was a civilian and there wasn't much he could do about me. "We know your work," he said stiffly, "and know that you are better equipped to work on a matter such as this than the average insurance investigator."

"I gather," I said, "that you also think your electronics case is related to the two other industrial espionage cases?"

He nodded. "We have no proof, but we think so."

"All right," I said. "You've given me everything you have?"

"Everything I can."

"What about your own investigation?" I asked.

"We're continuing it, of course—here and in Europe. It is important enough so that we have assigned several men to it."

"Am I to be told who they are?"

"You know better than that, Milo," he said reprovingly. "The agents themselves don't know what other men are assigned."

"Great," I said. "There'll be twenty or thirty of us chasing each other around while the real villain skips merrily on his way. That's the good old Army method."

He scowled. "You know damn well we can't work it any other way. One slip and the whole bunch could be wiped out."

"It might be a good idea," I said. "Okay, General. I'm used to it. You play it your way and I'll play it mine. But don't come around crying if some of your boys get hurt."

"Major March—" he started in anger; then he realized that I was a major only in the Reserves and he hadn't called me back to active duty. He restrained himself with effort. "Milo, my boy, you of all people understand my position."

"Sure," I said wearily. "I understood your position when you were a chicken colonel in France years ago. Okay, General, I'll do my best. Just tell your boys to protect themselves in the clinches. I'll see you around the officers' club."

I didn't wait for an answer. I got up and left the conference room before I said something I'd be sorry about.

When I reached the street I went into the nearest bar and had two fast martinis just for my morale. This was the "prize" job of all those that Martin Raymond had handed me. But I had fifty $100 bills in my pocket and I couldn't afford to give them back. So I had a job.

After the two martinis I took a cab to my apartment on Perry Street in Greenwich Village. I made some coffee and sat down to look at the file—what little there was of it. Actually, there wasn't much more than what I had been told. There were addresses for the three companies. Santee Chemical and Crossen Plastics were both in Philadelphia. There was nothing more except the dates of the suicides and the accidents and the addresses of the victims.

I decided I'd check on the top-secret place first. I packed some clothes and took a cab to a car rental agency I often used. I rented a car and headed for Connecticut. It was midafternoon when I arrived. I went directly to the Concord Hotel and parked in front of it. Inside, after some argument with the clerk, I was finally shown into the office of the manager. I showed him my identification. He looked at it for a full two minutes, then handed it back to me.

"What can I do for you, Mr. March?" he asked. His tone of voice indicated that he didn't really want to know what he could do for me.

"I don't know," I said honestly. "Our insurance company had a policy on an Angus Watson, who has disappeared, as you probably know, since he disappeared from your hotel. He had a meeting with a C. Jackson, who was registered here, and he has never been seen since. Neither, I understand, has Mr. Jackson."

"I know," he said wearily. "I've answered several times all the questions you could possibly think of, and those answers are a part of the police records. Why don't you check them?"

"I might do that," I said. "But I'd like to hear the answers from you also."

He leaned back and sighed. "All right, Mr. March. Mr. Jackson checked in here three days before the—ah—incident to which you refer. He rented a three-room suite, telling us he was here to interview job applicants. I believe that he placed an ad in the local paper the same day. He interviewed several men, and Mr. Watson was, so far as we know, the last one he interviewed. One of our bellboys saw Mr. Watson enter the waiting room. A few minutes later, a previous applicant left. Neither Mr. Watson nor Mr. Jackson was seen after that by any of our employees. I'm afraid that's all I can tell you."

"I never expect miracles," I told him. "Did you see Mr. Jackson yourself?"

"Yes." It was a reluctant admission.

"I know you have described him before," I said, "but would you mind doing it once more for me?"

He sighed again. "All right. He was about five feet eight or nine, maybe a hundred and seventy-five pounds, dark hair and eyes, pinkish face. He spoke very well and seemed to be an educated man. He was very pleasant, paid in advance for the suite, and tipped well."

"When he registered, did he indicate that he represented a company?"

"Yes. The Jackson Professional Services, Incorporated. He gave a New York address for the company. Would you like it?"

"Yes."

He went through a card file on his desk, found the right one, and copied the address down for me.

"I understand from the local police," he said, "that Jackson's home address is nonexistent. I don't know about this one."

"All right," I said. "Now, tell me how it is possible for two men to leave the hotel and not be seen by anyone."

"I suppose," he said, "that it would be possible for them to walk out through the lobby and not be noticed if we were very busy."

"Are you usually that busy?"

"No. They could also have taken the self-service elevator to the basement and gone out through the service entrance. It is doubtful if they would have been seen."

"Do you know what time this was, approximately?"

"Sometime between three-thirty and four-thirty. The previous applicant left the suite at three-thirty, and there was a call for Mr. Jackson at four-thirty, which was not answered."

"Who made the call?"

"Another applicant. The police have his name."

"That is all you can tell me?"

"That's it. So far I've told it to the local police, the state police, Federal officers, and a man from the CIA. It's still the same story."

"Well, it's been fun," I said. "Thanks."

I left the office, found the self-service elevator and took it to the basement, and wandered through it to the exit in the rear without seeing anyone. The back door opened on a small tar-surfaced area that was obviously meant for deliveries. I went back and checked the basement. There was still no one in sight. There were baskets of laundry waiting to be picked up, and all of the various machinery seemed to be working properly, but there were no workers in sight. If this was a normal situation, then it would certainly be easy for a dozen people to sneak out. I also checked to see if there were any other exits, but there was only the one.

When I was finally satisfied that there was nothing more to be learned there, I headed for the door. I stepped outside, intending to walk up to the street and my car.

I heard the sound of a step behind me, but not quickly enough. Something hard was shoved into my back. I'd had enough experience to know what it was—a gun.

"Take it easy," a voice said behind me. "Just do as we tell you and you won't be hurt."

TWO

He had said "we," so even as I was raising my hands I was looking around. He was to my left. He was a young, nice-looking man, wearing a Madison Avenue suit and holding a Third Avenue gun—a snub-nosed .38. There was something familiar-looking about him. In the meantime, the other one was frisking me.

"He's not armed," he finally said in surprise. He nudged me with the gun. "All right. Turn around—slowly."

I turned around, bringing my hands down. He was a replica of the other one I had seen. He was also holding a gun, pointed at my belt buckle.

"Who are you?" he asked.

"Look in my left coat pocket," I said.

He switched the gun to his left hand and reached into my pocket. "Cover him, Anderson," he said. He looked at my identification. All it said was that I represented the Intercontinental Insurance Company; my private detective's license was in another pocket.

"An insurance man," he said in disgust. "What are you doing here?"

"The hotel's policy is up for renewal," I said. "We have to check everything, including the basement exits." I already had an idea about them; I'd seen too many. "It's standard procedure. You ought to know that if you're local cops. You are, aren't you?"

"Not exactly," he said. He put his gun away. "All right, Anderson. I guess we drew a blank. We might as well forget about it."

The other man put his gun back in its holster and came down to where we stood.

Both of them looked slightly foolish and I was sure that my idea was right.

"What's this all about?" I said. I had decided to play the indignant citizen for a moment. "A guy is just doing his job and suddenly somebody jams a gun in his back. What's going on around here?"

"None of your business," the first man said sharply.

"What do you mean it's none of my business?" I demanded. "Obviously there is something wrong about this hotel, and my company has a lot of money at stake. I want to know what's going on."

"Take it easy, Mac," the second man said. "This is something too big for you. Just run along and write your little policies."

That convinced me. It also gave me a slow burn. The two of them were standing in front of me, almost shoulder to shoulder, and their guns were safely in their shoulder holsters. I decided it was better if they learned the facts of life from me than someone else.

"Well," I said, "it doesn't sound right …"

With that I hit the one on my left. It was a good, hard blow to the point of his chin, and I could feel it tingle all the way to my shoulder, so I knew that I didn't have to worry about him for a few minutes. I swung and kicked the other one on the kneecap. He bent over in pain. I clasped my hands and brought them down on his head, at the same time bringing my knee up to crash into his face. He groaned and collapsed beside his partner.

I took their two guns. Then I looked at their identification. On the surface it didn't mean anything. One was apparently a private detective, the other a special guard for Palmieri-Foster. Their names were supposedly Cooper and Anderson. I put their cards back, slipped one of the guns into my pocket, and waited for them to recover.

It took them about two minutes. Then they began to groan. One of them had a sore jaw and the other a bloody face. They took a look at the gun in my hand and got slowly to their feet.

"So you're not just an insurance man," the first one said.

"Sure I am," I said cheerfully, "but I get irritable when anyone shoves a gun in my back. I think I can prove that I'm just an insurance man."

"How?"

"Ever hear of a man named General Sam Roberts?" I asked.

They tried to pretend they hadn't, but there was enough reaction to prove to me that I was right. I smiled at them. "All right," I said. "Put your hands in your pockets and turn around. Walk very carefully ahead of me. We're going up to the street and to the first public phone booth on the street. Walk carefully. I was trained in a tougher time than you, and I was taught to shoot if there's any question at all. So be careful until I find out if my guess is right."

They put their hands in their pockets and turned to walk

side by side toward the street. I followed, and as we neared the street I put the gun in my pocket.

There was a phone booth a block away. We walked slowly and carefully to it. I had them stop and stand facing the booth while I stepped inside. I left the door open and used my left hand to get money from my pocket. My guess was that General Roberts had gone directly back to Washington after talking to me, so I called a special number in that city. It was a direct line and it was the General who answered.

"Hello, General," I said. "This is Milo March."

"What do you want?" he demanded.

"You know a couple of boys named Cooper and Anderson?"

"What if I do?" he demanded.

"One of them stuck a gun in my back. That was his first mistake. His second mistake was to put the gun back in his pocket without identifying himself. His friend did the same thing. So now I have both guns and both men. It's an embarrassment of riches. You want to talk to either one of them?"

"Cooper," he said gruffly.

"And may I suggest," I said, "that you ease up on the cloak-and-dagger bit enough to at least tell your various men about me. I don't like having guns stuck in my back. Hold on." I stepped out of the phone booth and motioned to Cooper. "He wants to talk to you."

Cooper didn't look too happy about it, but he stepped into the booth and picked up the receiver. I could hear his end of the conversation, but there wasn't much to it. He said "Yes, sir" five times and "No, sir" once. Then he hung up and came out with a sheepish expression.

"Sorry, Mr. March," he said.

"It's all right," I said. I handed them their guns. "But I suggest that the next time you make more certain of your prey before you put away your guns. Or perhaps take a refresher course back in Washington."

"Why didn't you tell us who you were?" Cooper asked.

"I did. I'm an insurance detective. What I've been in the past has nothing to do with it. And I didn't pull a gun; you did. If you point a gun at a man, he naturally wants to know why. So you should have told me who you were."

"You know we can't do that."

"I suppose so," I said, "but it might save a few broken bones and a lot of bruises. Anyway, I've asked the General to notify everyone working on this case that I'm in on it, too. It might save some trouble later on—if he does it. I suppose you fellows are covering this hotel just in case something turns up?"

They exchanged glances, and then Cooper decided to give an answer. "Yes," he said, but he bit the word off in a manner that indicated he wouldn't say any more.

"I get the message," I told him. "That's the only question you will answer. Okay. I don't mind doing my own work. Good luck, fellows." I turned and walked back down the street to my car. The two CIA men were still standing beside the phone booth as I drove by them.

I found the Palmieri-Foster factory without any trouble. Getting in to see the plant manager was another story.

There was a long conference between the guards, and one of them made two phone calls. He finally motioned me to follow him and led the way into the factory, past more guards, and finally stopped in front of a door which bore the name C. L. Young. He knocked on the door, and a voice on the other side murmured an invitation. The guard opened the door.

"This is Mr. March, sir," he said.

"Thank you," the man said. "Come in, Mr. March."

I went into the office and looked down at the gray-haired man behind the desk.

"It was nice of you to see me," I said with a touch of irony in my voice. "Intercontinental is always happy to know that their policyholders cooperate."

He leaned back in his chair. "Mr. March, I had a phone call telling me that you would undoubtedly appear. I was also told that you have a high clearance rating, otherwise you would never have gotten past the gate. What do you want?"

"Intercontinental carries the policy on your plant. We also carried a life policy on Angus Watson—who seems to be missing. I believe that the plant policy covers such things as missing equipment, and I understand that this was also involved in the disappearance of Mr. Watson. Now, Intercontinental has an understandable reluctance to pay out large sums of money, and if they have to, then they like to clean it up so as to discourage other people who might have similar ideas."

"Have you read the policies, Mr. March?" he asked.

"No, but I've been given at least some of the pertinent facts."

"I believe you will find all the proper clauses which prove that your company was well aware of certain limitations in insuring us and that they accepted those limitations."

"Including not talking?"

"Including that." He leaned further back in his chair. "I am at liberty to tell you this much and no more. We did have an engineer here by the name of Angus Watson. He recently went to the Concord Hotel to meet a man who had advertised that he wanted to hire electronics engineers. Mr. Watson was asked to sound out the intentions of the advertiser. What was not known at the time was that Mr. Watson had in his pocket a model of a very new electronics device which he had invented. Neither Mr. Watson nor the model has been seen since he entered the suite in the hotel."

"I understand that a few other men answered the ad. Were any of them from here?"

"All of them. But Mr. Jackson showed little interest in them, for none of them were employed on top-secret work or knew anything about it."

"Did they all come back and voluntarily report their experience?"

"No comment."

"Two more questions," I said, "and then I'll leave you to your little secrets. How was it possible for Angus Watson to walk out of here with the device in his pocket?"

He hesitated a moment. "Our regular procedure had been relaxed somewhat in the case of Angus Watson. We discovered that Watson did some of his best work at home or while walking around. After checking with Washington, it was agreed to let him carry some of his work with him. The device in question was, we thought, an almost perfect invention. But Angus thought he could improve it. I guess he'd been carrying it with him for weeks and thought nothing of keeping it in his pocket."

"You know," I said softly, "even though I haven't read the policy you have, I think it might contain a little clause in there somewhere about negligence. Intercontinental didn't arrive where they are by being simple-minded. And it would seem to me that permitting an employee—even an Angus Watson—to walk out of here with a highly secret and valuable gadget could be considered an act of negligence."

He looked startled. "I—I don't know about such a clause."

"You'll find it there," I said cheerfully. "Insurance companies like to feel that the policyholder is going to take reasonable care of the object being insured."

"What do you want, Mr. March?" he asked wearily.

"Just stop trying to sweep me under the rug," I told him. "I know that there are many things you can't talk about, but a description of the gadget invented by Angus Watson wouldn't help me a damn bit to find it or him. The things I do need to know can hardly be classified as top secret, and certainly can't be kept that way if you try. In the meantime, it might help if you and Washington both keep remembering that you are asking me—directly or indirectly—to rescue your precious secret. You do that and I might succeed. But if everyone is going to fight me every step of the way, I might as well go home and knit myself a pair of socks."

"All right, Mr. March," he said. "I apologize. It is an unusual situation, and I'm afraid everyone's nerves are a little ragged. I was also told that you had a good understanding of top-secret precautions. I believe you said you wanted to ask two more questions. You've only asked one of them."

"I hadn't forgotten. It seems to me that it would not be easy to force a man out of the hotel and out of town without being seen by someone. Do you think that Angus Watson might have gone along with this Jackson voluntarily?"

"Absolutely not. There is no question of his loyalty. There would be none in my mind anyway, but the government has had him under a magnifying glass for years."

"I wasn't questioning his loyalty or even suggesting that he would do it for money. There are many other possibilities. Maybe something was held over his head or his wife's. Maybe there was some sort of threat against his wife or his children, if he has any."

"He has two children. But you must be aware, Mr. March, that if there were so much as a flyspeck of a suspicious nature in the life of Angus Watson or his wife, the government would have found it."

"They've missed a few flyspecks," I said. "Not many, but a few."

"In addition," he continued, "I've known Angus Watson most of his life. He has worked here since he graduated from college. I know his wife and I know his children. I would stake my life that there is nothing about any of them that could be used against them. And since Angus started doing some of his work at home, there has been a constant guard on duty, so there would be very little chance of anyone doing anything to his family."

"What about relatives in Europe?"

"If there are any, they are very distant. Angus is an eighth-generation American, and his wife is seventh. You're on the wrong track. You can be sure that Angus Watson was kidnapped, perhaps murdered."

"How?" I asked.

"How? How the hell should I know? That's your job. Mine is to make—ah—" He stopped as he realized he had been on the point of mentioning forbidden subjects.

"Things," I finished for him. I stood up. "And mine is to find … things. By myself, obviously."

As I walked out of his office, the guard immediately fell into step beside me and escorted me out of the building and to the gate.

"I don't know how I would have made it without you," I told him. "I'll ask for you the next time I'm up this way." I patted him on the cheek and left.

I looked up Angus Watson's address and took a taxi to it. I told the driver to wait. It's just as well that I did. I got within about ten feet of the door when a man stepped around the corner of the house.

"Where do you think you're going?" he asked.

"Just stopping off for my weekly dancing lesson," I said brightly. "Are you the new teacher?"

"A wise guy," he said. He lumbered nearer. His right hand was inside his coat and I didn't doubt there was a gun there. "Who are you? And don't give me any smart answers."

"I wouldn't think of it," I told him. "I wouldn't want to confuse you. I'm Milo March."

He relaxed some but not very much. "I've heard of you. The insurance dick."

"Word does get around, doesn't it?"

"If you had some idea of seeing Mrs. Watson," he continued, "you can forget it. Nobody's allowed to see her, that's my orders and that's the way it's going to be."

"Who do you work for—local or Federal?"

"None of your business. Just get back in your taxi and take off."

"From the amount of cooperation I'm getting," I said, "I'm beginning to wonder if the whole thing isn't a local crime. I'll see you around, Cecil."

He was glaring at me as I went back to the taxi. I told the driver to take me to the police station.

After a short wait, I got in to see the chief. His name was Homer Grant. He looked capable enough, but that didn't necessarily mean too much. I showed him my Intercontinental identification.

"Let me guess what you want," he said sourly. "You're here about Angus Watson."

"That's right."

"I wish you luck," he said. He leaned back in his chair. "I've been a cop all my life. Right here. We don't have many cases this big, I guess, but I've never had a case before where I was made to feel that my proper job was to escort old ladies across the street."

"You mean you haven't been able to work on your own case?"

"I'm not sure you can call it work," he said bitterly. "We've been allowed to tag along and watch other people work. Most of the time we've been busy trying to comb FBI men, CIA men, and even plant guards out of our hair. Once in a while some of my men can sneak off and try to do something on their own, but I'm afraid we haven't come up with much."

"Watson disappeared six weeks ago Wednesday. Any idea how he and this Jackson got out of town, not to mention the hotel, without being seen?"

"Not the slightest," Grant admitted. "Neither do they. One of those smart-pants Federal cops followed Watson to the hotel and was outside all the time, and he didn't see them leave."

"But they left."

"They left, all right. This is not a large city, Mr. March. It's not like it was New York or Chicago. Everything has been checked. We know that Jackson arrived by train and took a taxi to the hotel. We've checked all the taxi drivers. They didn't leave by taxi. There are two car rental agencies in town. They didn't rent a car. They didn't buy a car. They didn't leave on foot. Even if that Federal cop was asleep, somebody would've noticed them. Angus Watson was well known in town. Every stranger who was in town at the time has been accounted for. I didn't do it personally, but they were checked and rechecked by the bright boys from Washington. I suppose they know their jobs."

"Maybe a cab driver was paid enough to make him keep his mouth shut?"

He shook his head. "I won't say that every driver in town would turn in your wallet if you lost it in his cab, but they'd talk once they discovered what this was about. Besides, none of them is smart enough or tough enough to stand up under prolonged questioning. And that they got. In addition, the government man who followed Watson said that only one taxi came to the hotel during that period. It came to pick up a little old lady who took a train to New York."

"She left by herself?"

"Yes. And she was also checked out. Angus Watson certainly did not leave with that man Jackson voluntarily. He was about five-eleven, maybe a hundred and seventy-five pounds. It would have been almost impossible to disguise him as anything and get him out of the hotel without his being noticed."

"I'm glad you said almost," I murmured, "because it happened. I forgot to ask at the hotel. What floor were Jackson's rooms on?"

"The fourth—and in the front, so they didn't drop out of the window."

"That's nice. I also understand that Jackson left no fingerprints behind?"

"Not any that have been found, and I guess they looked pretty hard."

"A locked room ..."

"What?"

"I was talking to myself," I said. "Years ago there was a passion for what was called locked-room detective stories. A crime took place in a room which to all intents and purposes was locked on the inside. Either it was completely locked or was watched so closely that it was the same thing. Do you suppose our Mr. Jackson is addicted to detective stories?"

"He's probably more practical than that," the Chief said. "He reads his bank account, I'll bet."

"Yeah," I said. "Well, thanks, Chief."

I stopped in front of the police station and thought about the case. Obviously I wasn't going to learn much more in that town. But one idea was nagging at me, and I decided another cab wouldn't hurt.

I took a cab back to the hotel. I noticed the two CIA men were still outside as I went in to see the manager again.

"I just want to know a couple of things," I told him, "and then I won't bother you again. Who takes care of the laundry and ordering supplies and accepting deliveries?"

"Well, the list for supplies for the rooms is made up by the housekeeper. It is checked by me and then the order is placed. The same method is used by the chef for the dining room. Laundry is placed in large bags and taken to the basement, where it is picked up once a week. All deliveries are made through the basement and are accepted by Mr. McIntosh, who is in charge of maintenance. He has an office next to the furnace room."

I thanked him and went to the basement again. It took me a little time, but I finally found the tiny office. The man who sat in it was so big he seemed to fill the entire room. He looked up as I stopped in the doorway.

"Mr. McIntosh?" I asked.

He nodded.

"I'm from the Intercontinental Insurance Company. The manager said I could ask you a couple of questions."

He nodded again and waited.

"You accept all the deliveries for the hotel?"

"Yes."

"Are there special days for such deliveries?"

"Depends. Kitchen supplies are delivered on Tuesdays and Saturdays. Laundry is picked up every Wednesday and delivered every Monday. Other supplies are delivered as ordered, usually the day after the order is placed."

"Where are they delivered?"

"Well, supplies for the rooms go to the storage room down here. Kitchen supplies are taken up to the kitchen. General maintenance supplies go into the supply room down here."

"You check the deliveries and sign for them?"

"Yes."

"What about the laundry?"

"It goes to the second floor, and the housekeeper sees it is distributed to the linen closets on each floor."

"What about the outgoing laundry?"

"When the rooms are changed, the linen is placed in large bags on each floor.

Early each Wednesday morning they're brought down here to the corridor to be picked up by the laundry."

"Any special time for the pickup?"

He shook his head. "Anytime from noon to five o'clock. Whenever they get here."

"Do you also oversee that?"

He looked surprised. "No. It isn't necessary."

"How many bags of laundry go out each week?"

"It depends. If the hotel is full, there will be six bags. Sometimes there are no more than two."

"And you don't have to check them out? What if the laundry doesn't return everything?"

"They always have. Hotel's used the same laundry since I've been here, and that's fifteen years. Never been anything missing that I heard of."

"What laundry?"

"Peerless—on Fourth Street."

"Thanks," I said.

I went back to the main room and out the front door. I looked around until I spotted the two CIA men. I walked over to them.

"Catch any more suspicious characters?" I asked.

"What do you want, March?" Cooper asked.

"I want to ask a couple of questions which do not involve security. Will you answer them, or do I have to call the General in Washington?"

"Ask them and we'll see," Cooper said.

"Who was following Angus Watson that day he came here to meet Jackson?"

He thought about it for a minute. "We did," he said finally.

"I know that you've stated you did not see Watson or Jackson leaving the hotel. I suppose it was impossible to sneak them out the front door, but what about the back? Deliveries and pickups are made through that entrance."

"I'm well aware of it," Cooper said stiffly. "I was watching the rear entrance. During the time involved, there was one pickup—the laundry."

"What time?"

"Shortly before four o'clock."

"I suppose you checked him?" I asked.

"Naturally. Although we did not then know that Watson was in any danger, I stopped the truck. It was a Peerless Laundry Company truck. I kept it there while Anderson checked inside to see if their laundry was done by Peerless and what day it was generally picked up."

"That's all?"

He was angry but he tried not to show it. "No. I checked the truck's registration, and it was in order. I also checked the interior of the truck, which was half full of laundry bags. The driver carried a card in the Teamsters Union, and Anderson called Peerless and checked him out. Then I let him pick up the laundry."

"Did you watch him?"

"Of course."

"How about the two men slipping into the truck while the driver was loading laundry?"

"Impossible. The back of his truck was at least three feet from the rear door of the hotel. I watched as he loaded and continued to watch as the driver closed the doors and drove away."

"How many bags of laundry?"

"Four."

"What time did you leave here?"

"Shortly after four-thirty when we were notified that no one answered Jackson's phone. We called in and went immediately to the rooms on the fourth floor. We were there for at least two hours."

"Thank you," I said gravely.

"General Roberts's orders," he said. "I was told to cooperate with you as long as it did not involve any matters of security."

I nodded and turned away. This time I picked up my rented car where I had parked it and drove off. It wasn't too hard to find Fourth Street and the Peerless Laundry. I parked and went in. I asked to see the manager. When he came in, I showed him my identity.

"You do the laundry for the Concord Hotel?" I asked.

"Ever since it was built," he said, "seventeen years ago. Is there anything wrong?"

"If you mean with the service, no. When do you pick up the laundry at the hotel?"

"The middle of the week, I believe. I'll look it up." He took a thick book from beneath the counter and leafed through it. Finally he stopped at a page. He nodded. "Yes. We pick up there on Wednesday."

"And did you pick up as usual on Wednesday six weeks ago?"

He looked at me for a minute. "Ah," he said, "the day that Angus Watson disappeared." He looked at the book. "Yes, we picked up that day."

"How many bags of laundry?"

He checked the book again. "Four."

I was about to turn away when I had another thought. I looked back at him.

"Does your book show what time the pickup was made that day?"

"Certainly." He looked down again until he found what he wanted. "He picked up the laundry at five o'clock." He stopped and seemed to be trying to remember something. "You know," he said," something funny happened that day. I just remembered it. About four o'clock a man called and said he was a government agent. He wanted to know if we had a driver named Frank Nabor who drove the truck that picked up laundry at the hotel. I guess he must've found out the laundry was to be picked up and wanted to make sure it was our driver when he arrived."

THREE

There was a moment of elation, which always comes when you finally see a ray of light, but I did not let it show. What he said meant that there had been two trucks at the hotel that day marked with the name of Peerless and two drivers with identical names. It was obviously something that no one else had yet discovered, and I was not about to share it. If they were going to have top secrets, I would have a few of my own.

"I imagine so," I told the laundry manager. "They are very thorough about those things. Well, thank you."

"Glad to help," he said.

When I was outside I looked for the nearest phone booth. I called the hotel and asked for the manager.

"This is Milo March again," I said when he came on. "I'm sorry to bother you once more, but if you will find the answer to two questions for me, I won't bother you again."

"All right," he said. He sounded tired. "If I can. What is it?"

"I'll stay on the phone. Call your housekeeper and see if she remembers or has a record of how many bags of laundry were sent out six weeks ago. And one other thing. You mentioned that a call came in for Mr. Jackson that Wednesday and that was how you discovered they were gone. But would you check and see if Mr. Jackson made any calls during that period, and if so, to what number?"

"I don't understand," he said.

"You don't have to," I answered. "And I'll never bother you again."

"Very well," he said.

I waited, feeding coins into the phone when the operator told me my time was up. Finally he came back on the phone.

"The housekeeper says that six bags of laundry were sent out on that Wednesday. And Mr. Jackson did make one phone call that afternoon, at three-thirty. The number he called was Home 3-3962. You realize, Mr. March, I'll have to tell the government men about this call and the information I gave you?"

"Of course," I said cheerfully. "I expect you to do so. It's the patriotic duty of every man. Good-bye."

I hung up and waited a minute. Then I dropped in another coin and dialed the number the manager had given me. The phone rang and rang. I was about to give up when a man answered.

"Who am I speaking to?" I asked.

"I don't know who you want," he said irritably, "but I think you've got the wrong number. This is a public phone booth outside of my gas station." He hung up.

I got into my car and drove thoughtfully toward New York City. When I reached the city I stopped long enough to see if I had any mail and to check with my answering service. The results were negative on both counts. I got back into the car and headed for Philadelphia.

As soon as I got there, I stopped and looked up Crossen Plastics and Santee Chemical. They were more or less in the same area. I drove to that section and checked into a motel. It was too late to visit the companies, so I found a nearby restaurant and enjoyed a couple of martinis and a fine Italian dinner. Then I picked up the newspapers and a bottle of V.O. I went back to the motel, got a bucket of cubes from the ice machine, made myself a king-size drink, and stretched out on the bed.

There wasn't much in the papers, so I finally undressed, turned on the television, and got in bed. Halfway through my second drink, while some guy on television was chasing another guy through a swamp, I fell asleep before I could get up enough energy to switch off the TV or the light.

The morning show was on when I awakened. It didn't seem very exciting at the moment, so I turned it off and took a shower. The motel had something which they called "courtesy coffee"—a hot water dispenser, packaged instant coffee, cream and sugar, and a cup. I made some coffee, poured out a moderate drink of V.O., and sipped them alternately while I tried to adjust to the fact that it was a new day. When I finally accepted this bit of wisdom, I got dressed and went out to have some breakfast.

The Crossen Plastics company looked like dozens of other modern factories which have sprung up in the last twenty years. Everything was gleaming and modern, surrounded by well-trimmed grass and mathematically arranged flowers. But in other respects it reminded me of the factory in Connecticut. I was stopped at the gate by a security guard.

He listened gravely to my story and then went to the phone, while I stood outside the iron gate trying to look nonchalant.

Finally he came back and said that I could see a Mr. James David. He summoned another guard before he opened the gate, and the second one escorted me through a number of confusing corridors and finally stopped in front of a handsome oak door. There was no nameplate on it, so I guessed that Mr. David was an important man. The guard motioned for me to go in.

The reception room was as large as most offices and was tastefully furnished—with a beautiful blonde. She made an effort and tore her gaze away from the polish on her nails to look at me.

"Yes?" she asked in a voice only slightly colder than that of an unloving mother-in-law.

"I'm Milo March," I said. "I was told that a Mr. David had consented to see me. You must have been expecting me— unless the guard at the gate dialed the wrong number."

"Oh, yes. Mr. David said that he would see you as soon as you arrived. This way, please." She stood up and moved—or rather, flowed—toward another highly polished door. The only part of her that moved was her feet. The rest of her couldn't have moved if it tried. She wasn't wearing a living girdle;* rigor mortis had already started.

She opened the door. "Mr. March is here, Mr. David," she said.

"Send him right in," a hearty voice said from somewhere out of sight.

---

* A reference to the Playtex Living Girdle, which had been sold since the 1940s. By the later '60s (this book was published in 1965), pantyhose were more popular among women than stockings attached to girdles, though perhaps no less unattractive to men. (All footnotes were added by the editor.)

The blonde held the door open and stepped back, standing rigidly straight with her gaze fixed somewhere over my head. I almost saluted as I passed her.

The private office had the rich simplicity that you sometimes see on Madison Avenue. It had a wall-to-wall rug that was at least three inches thick. There were two handsome leather chairs, something against the wall that looked suspiciously like a camouflaged bar, and a desk that was at least ten feet long. The desk was clean. The man who sat behind it was as handsome as the room. He had the look of a former football star who had grown rich and acquired distinguished gray hair in the process.

"Hello, Mr. March," he said in that same hearty voice. "Please sit down." He motioned to one of the leather chairs near his desk. It was going to be an intimate conversation.

I took the chair and looked at him. "This is very interesting," I said. "I merely told the guard at the gate my name, that I was from Intercontinental Insurance, and that I wanted to talk to someone about several of your insurance policies. In a place as heavily guarded as this is, that should have earned me a bum's rush. Instead I was escorted here by a man and what looked like a forty-five caliber gun. And I doubt very much if you're the man who handles insurance policies."

He laughed. "You're right, Mr. March. I am the executive vice-president of Crossen Plastics. And, frankly, I was told that you'd probably be around and that it would be better to see you or you might react—unfavorably."

So he was going to be frank about everything. That was always a dangerous sign.

"Who told you that? Washington?"

"Yes," he admitted. He beamed at me as though we were two Rotarians who had just met in the middle of a desert. "We do have security problems here since we do a certain amount of classified work for the government and have to take precautions. But I was told that you also have a high security rating—and that you are persistent."

"Did they also tell you that they're hoping I'll solve all their little problems for them?"

"I—I don't understand."

"Sure you do. You didn't get to be executive vice-president by not understanding buck-passing."

He cleared his throat and decided to change the subject. "What can I do for you, Mr. March?"

"You know the answer to that, too," I said. "But if you want to play a game, I'll take a short walk through the dream garden with you—a very short one. Intercontinental Insurance issued policies against the theft of important inventions belonging to this company. It also issued life insurance policies, with double-indemnity clauses, on two of your employees—Richard Matson and Carl Kelly. They are no longer with us. Unfortunate accidents, we are told."

"Yes," he said gravely. "It was very unfortunate."

"That is our view of the matter, too," I said. "I hate to bring it up, but there is a small matter of two missing inventions which have already shown up on the European market. That will also cost us a pretty penny. Not that we regret this much more than we would the collapse of our building in New York, but we take a dim view of anyone else being encouraged by this success. I'm sure you can understand that."

"Of course," he said. He turned his chair so that he wouldn't have to look directly at me. "I repeat, Mr. March, what can I do for you?"

"Talk."

"It might be better if you asked me what you wanted to know, Mr. March."

Some of the heartiness had left his voice.

"All right. Let's start with the two men—Matson and Kelly. What did they do here?"

"They were both engineers—valuable ones."

"Had they worked on the two inventions which were stolen and have since shown up in Europe?"

"Yes."

"What were the inventions?"

"I cannot give you details," he said, "but one was a plastic which was stronger, and cheaper, than steel. The other was a plastic capable of resisting enormous amounts of heat. The government was interested in both processes. Matson and Kelly were completely responsible for both."

"Had they been working in recent times on other inventions?"

He hesitated for a long minute. "Yes," he said finally. "We have not as yet made a complete report to your company, but they had completed one other process which, apparently, was also stolen."

"What was it?"

"I cannot tell you. I have very strict orders on that. All I can say is that it is something which can play an important role in our space program."

"Has it also shown up in Europe?"

"Not that we know of. It is possible that whoever has it is looking for the highest bidder."

"Any doubt that Matson and Kelly did steal the processes?"

"No," he said sadly. "I don't understand it. But everything here has been checked over and over, and there is no doubt that they did it. I don't know why. They received extremely good salaries and bonuses, and had great futures with the company. They both had been cleared, and up to this there was no doubt of their loyalty."

"Any other reasons why they might have done it?"

"Not that I know of."

"Did they have any new acquaintances in the period just before the thefts?"

"Again, I wouldn't know. Maybe the investigating officers …"

"Sure," I said. "If I ask one of them the time of day, all he'd do would be to make sure I hadn't stolen his watch. I'm supposed to do their work, but with a blindfold on."

He looked uncomfortable.

"All right," I said. "What about the accidents?"

"Just accidents—I guess." He didn't look too sure about it.

"You guess? Doesn't anyone ever tell you anything?"

"Not very much," he admitted, "not on that end of things. But the official verdict is that both were killed in accidents."

"Whose official verdict?"

"The story was given to the newspapers by a Captain Shaffner of Homicide."

"Who investigated for the government?"

"I don't know."

I'd been annoyed with him; now I was beginning to feel sorry for him. "Don't worry about it," I told him. "They always act as if there was a strange kid on the block who was going to steal their candy. Is there anything else you can tell me about the case?"

"I'm afraid not, Mr. March. I'm sorry."

"Well, it's been fun," I said. I stood up. Then I looked down at him. He was beginning to look like a football player who had run the wrong way with the ball. "Did you ever hear of a man named Jackson?"

He shook his head. "I don't recall the name. Why?"

"Just curiosity. Thank you for your time, Mr. David." I turned and left the office.

The receptionist was busy examining her fingernails again.

I stopped in front of her desk. "It must keep you very busy," I said.

She looked up. "What?"

"The polish on your nails," I said solemnly. "Personally, I would suggest a much brighter red."

This time her eyebrows moved—up. "Really?" she said.

I nodded. "Someone as pretty as you ought to give some external evidence of being a red-blooded woman—especially in a place where everything is made out of plastic."

For a second there was a flicker in her eyes, then they frosted over again. "Is that all, Mr. March?"

"No," I said cheerfully. "I may drop back to see if you've followed my advice. If not, I know some better tests to determine if you're a real woman or not. You may have possibilities you haven't dreamed of, so chin up, honey."

I smiled and left before she could think of anything to say.

The guard was waiting faithfully in the corridor to escort me back to the iron gate. Then both guards gazed suspiciously after me as I drove away.

The Santee Chemical Corporation proved to be quite different. Its building was just as modern, but there was no iron fence around it and no suspicious guards hanging around the front of the building. There was a guard inside the lobby, but he gave me only a casual glance and went back to the magazine he was reading.

There was also a receptionist on the main floor, a pretty little brunette who looked up with a smile as I approached her desk.

"Thank heavens," I said. "I'm back in civilization at last. I thought I'd never make it across that last stretch of sand."

Her smile got a little uncertain, but it remained. "I'm not sure I know what you're talking about," she said.

"I'm not either," I admitted. "I just came from Crossen Plastics, and I wasn't sure that the receptionist there wasn't also made out of plastic. I thought it might be a plague or an invasion from another planet. The sight of you just reassured me."

She laughed. "I've heard everyone over there is pretty grim. Whom did you wish to see?"

"It's not a question of my wishes," I said. "I have to see someone here, but I don't know who it is."

"What's it about?"

"That might help," I admitted. "My name is Milo March. I represent Intercontinental Insurance. We carry all of the insurance on this company and on many of the employees.

I am here in reference to some claims which are to be made against those policies."

"Oh, you must mean poor Mr. Halsey and Mr. Frame. That was terrible." She pursed her lips—a pretty sight. "I think maybe you ought to see Mr. Lamarr. What did you say your name was?"

"I was hoping you'd remember it longer than that," I said sadly. "It's Milo March."

She picked up her phone and punched a button. "There's a Mr. March here from our insurance company. He'd like to see Mr. Lamarr." She waited a couple of minutes, then said, "Thank you."

She looked up at me. "He'll see you, Mr. March. Take the elevator to the fourth floor, and it's the sixth office to the right as you get off the elevator."

I followed her advice and ended up in a small reception room occupied by another pretty and friendly girl. I told her who I was and she motioned to the only other door and told me to go in.

This private office was just as large as Henry's, with just as thick a rug on the floor, but there the similarity ended. There was an untidy look about this office, and the desk was piled high with papers. The man who stood up and held out his hand was a big, shaggy man with rumpled clothes.

"March," he said. "I'm Lamarr. Sit down. Have a cigar?"

"No, thanks," I said. "I'll stick to my cigarettes—in spite of all the warnings."*

* In the U.S., the Cigarette Labeling and Advertising Act required health warnings on cigarette packs, beginning in 1966. The legislation was passed the year this book was published, 1965. (All footnotes were added by the editor.)

He chuckled. "A fine way for an insurance man to talk. I suppose you're here about our thefts?"

"I'd like to ask a few questions," I admitted.

"I'll be glad to tell you everything I know," he said. "Shoot."

"If I look a little dazed," I said, "it's because I'm not used to such treatment. A couple of other policyholders, including one near here, have had similar experiences, and in both places I've been treated as if I were there to steal the rest of their secrets."

"They have government contracts?"

"Yes."

"Well, we don't. There's nothing classified about a cleaning fluid. Washington doesn't tell us what to do—except when it comes to taxes. I'll admit that for a while I was ass-deep in all sorts of government cops, but as soon as they discovered that we didn't have anything but strictly commercial secrets, they departed as quickly as they came. They never did let me know what they found out while they were working, so all I can tell you is what I know personally, but I'll be glad to do that."

"I'll try to pull myself together," I said. "What was stolen from your company?"

"A new cleaning fluid that surpassed anything on the market and could be sold for less money. A deodorant that was a big advance in that field. And a drug that was a real breakthrough in the treatment of arthritis. The latter was the most important—although probably not the most profitable. People will pay more to get rid of odors, good or bad, than to get rid of pain. The first two processes have already shown up in Europe. It won't kill our market here, but it will hurt us."

"Who is selling them in Europe?"

He shrugged. "Five or six companies, but that doesn't mean anything. They undoubtedly leased the processes from someone else. That is the usual procedure."

"Any ideas?"

"No. We can't even afford to try to trace it. When we find that something has been stolen by an American company, we can, and do, go to court, although that is a long and expensive maneuver. But when it goes to Europe, it's better to just forget about it unless they try to market it here. Some of those smart Washington boys—since they seem to think our thefts fit in with the others—might have an idea, but if they have, they didn't bother to tell me."

"What about the thefts? You know who took the processes?"

"Yes," he said gravely, "we know. I wish we didn't. They were taken by Robert Halsey and Dan Frame, two of the best men we ever had. And I liked them. Hell, I've been in both of their houses dozens of times, had dinner with them, played with their kids."

"How can you be so sure they did it?"

"The government isn't the only one in espionage these days," he said. "Big business is in it, too. We don't go in for iron fences and guards at the entrances, but you can be sure that we're careful about the floors where we have our labs and the manufacturing plant. Not only do we use guards, but also every electronic device that's been invented. Our labs are insulated so that if anyone succeeded in planting a microphone in them, its broadcast would not go through the walls. Every employee who has access has been checked out a dozen times. It had to be Halsey and Frame."

"Why did they do it?"

"I suppose it had to be money, although I don't know why. They made damned good money. Both of them owned better-than-average homes and the mortgages were paid."

"Any vices?"

"Not that I know of, and I knew them both very well. They were devoted husbands and fathers, and I doubt if they knew a horse from a cow or a pair of dice from cubes of sugar."

"And then they both committed suicide," I said, "within a period of two weeks. Why?"

"Again, I don't know, March. I can only guess. We make periodic checks on security measures without any advance notice. We had just started such a check and it's possible that they became frightened."

"Are you sure that they committed suicide?"

He looked surprised. "Are you suggesting something else?"

"I'm not suggesting anything. I'm asking a question."

"Of course they committed suicide," he said. "That was the official verdict. After all, they did have a sort of reason for suicide when they thought they were going to be caught. It couldn't have been anything else. Neither one of them had any enemies."

"That you know of," I suggested gently.

"What do you mean? You don't think they committed suicide?"

"I don't know what I think," I said. "It's just that everything is too damned neat, too convenient. I don't like things that are all wrapped and tied before you even get to them. Is there anything else you can tell me?"

He shook his head. "I don't think so. As I told you, no one told me anything."

"Who gave out the official verdict of suicide?"

"The local police. Captain Shaffner of Homicide. He's a good man, but he wouldn't answer any of my questions either. Maybe he'll tell you more."

"I'll try," I said. I stood up. "Can you give me the addresses of Halsey and Frame?"

"Ask my secretary," he said wearily. He seemed depressed by our conversation.

"Okay, thanks," I said.

I left him there, slumped behind the pile of papers on his desk.

The secretary wrote down the addresses for me, and I took the elevator down to the ground floor. I took another look at the receptionist and reluctantly went out to my car. Business before pleasure, I reminded myself firmly.

The Robert Halsey house was the nearest, and I drove to it. Lamarr had been right; it wasn't a cheap house. The well-kept lawn was bordered with flowers, and there was a hedge in front. A big, burly man was working on the hedge, although it didn't look as if it needed trimming.

I parked in front of the house and started up the walk. Suddenly the man was in front of me, the hedge shears swinging loosely in his left hand.

"Looking for somebody, buster?" he asked. There was nothing friendly about his voice or attitude.

FOUR

There was one thing certain; he was no gardener. In the first place, gardeners seldom challenge visitors, but are more apt to give them a toothy smile and go on with their pruning. Also, I had never met a gardener who carried a gun, since it's pretty difficult to hit a Japanese beetle with a .38. There was a bulge under this man's left arm, and I didn't think it was a tumor.

"Yes," I said politely. "I'm paying a social call on Mrs. Halsey. You may continue with your hedges, my good man."

"She's not seeing anyone," he said. He'd moved around so he was blocking the walk to the house.

"It seems to me," I said mildly, "that it's a decision that's up to Mrs. Halsey, not her gardener."

"You heard me. She's not seeing anyone."

"Do you have any authority?" I asked.

"My authority is that I'm telling you to get out," he said.

I didn't have any doubt what his authority was, but I was also getting tired of being pushed around.

"Oh, well," I said.

I started to turn and hit him. I missed the button, but I hit him hard enough to knock him down, the hedge shears flying from his hand.

Without trying to get up, he reached for the gun. I let him get it out of the holster and then I stepped on his hand. He let go of the gun and grunted with pain. He started to twist his body so he could grab my ankle with his other hand.

"I wouldn't," I said. "You'll need a complete dental job if you try."

He subsided and glared up at me. "Don't push your luck too far, March," he said.

I looked at him in mock surprise. "Ah, the man knows me. Now, I don't recall meeting any gardeners socially."

His face was red with anger. "My orders were not to arrest you, but you're making it difficult."

"Orders? From whom? The State Department of Conservation? But I haven't touched the hedge. If you have any other authority, I suggest that you identify it."

"Go to hell," he said.

I ground my foot down on his hand until he gritted his teeth with pain. "As of now," I said cheerfully, "you are merely an impudent gardener who is guilty of attempted assault with a deadly weapon. As a law-abiding citizen, I have a right to defend myself."

He continued to glare at me for several seconds, then the fight went out of him.

"All right," he said. He put his left hand in his pocket and came out with a leather folder and flipped it open. He was a government cop, all right.

"Well, well," I said. "They must be scraping the bottom of the barrel these days." I took my foot off his hand. "You can get up, retrieve your gun, and put it back in its holster. But I'd move very slowly if I were you. I'm allergic to having guns pointed at me, even by cops."

I stood back and waited. He got to his feet and picked up the gun. It was plain he was wishing he could use it, but he put it away and stared at me.

"Am I under arrest?" I asked sweetly.

"My orders were not to arrest you," he repeated. He sounded as if he were choking. "My orders also were that you were not to see Mrs. Halsey under any circumstances. If you persist in your attempts, I may then use my own judgment. I hope you try." He bit off the last four words as though he were spitting out a bad taste.

"If I try, I'll see her," I said quietly. "I am, however, perfectly willing to cooperate—which is more than I can say for any of your bunch. But I'm tired of being pushed around by a bunch of amateurs, and you may quote me in your report. If you'd identified yourself in the beginning, I would have left quietly. But don't throw your weight around; you don't weigh that much. What's the idea of sealing Mrs. Halsey off? Her husband wasn't involved with any classified material."

"I don't know," he said. "I just have my orders. Now get out of here."

"I suppose the same orders apply to Mrs. Frame?" I asked.

"Yes."

"Well, it's nice to see the taxpayers' money spent so wisely," I said. "Are you a gambling man, Percival?"

His face reddened again. "My name is Hayes," he said stiffly.

"I'll make you a bet," I told him. "You have a whole little army of smart boys, but I'll bet you ten bucks that I find the answer to all of this before you do."

"Get out," he said hoarsely.

"Sure. Give my regards to the boys—and I do mean boys—back in Washington." I went to my car and drove away.

Obviously there was little point in trying to see Mrs. Frame. I stopped at the first gas station and looked up the police department. I phoned and got the address of Homicide. It still wasn't quite lunchtime, so I drove directly to the building that housed Homicide.

I stepped up to the desk sergeant, a beefy individual who was a duplicate of twenty sergeants to be found at the desks of twenty city police departments. He looked at me with suspicion, as if he were certain I was there to confess I had just murdered my wife.

"I would like to see Captain Shaffner," I said.

It increased his suspicion. "What about?" he asked.

"My name is March," I said. I took out my identification and held it so he could see it. "I represent Intercontinental Insurance of New York. I am here in regard to a case with which Captain Shaffner is familiar. I'd like to talk to him about it for a few minutes, if he can spare the time."

The Sergeant wasn't impressed, but he knew better than to make a decision on his own. He picked up the phone and passed my words along to the Captain. When he hung up, his expression indicated that he wasn't too sure about the Captain's sanity.

"He'll see you," he said. "Go down that corridor. It's the second door on the right." He went back to examining what seemed to be the squeal book*—but I suspected that there was a comic book inside it.

---

* The daily record of complaints of crimes to the police.

I reached the second door on the right and knocked. A voice told me to come in. I opened the door and walked into a room filled with cigar smoke. It took a few seconds for my eyes to adjust, and then I saw the Captain seated at a battered old desk, puffing away at a cigar. An ashtray on the desk was filled with cigar butts, some of them still smoldering. The Captain was a little on the heavy side, but I was surprised to find him younger than I had expected. He seemed to be about my age, and I had a strange feeling that there was something familiar about him.

"Come in and shut the door," he said irritably.

"Too much fresh air?" I asked as I closed the door behind me.

"Everything happens in fresh air," he growled. "Did you ever hear of anyone being murdered in a smoke-filled room? No. It's always out in the open or in a nice, clean room. If the place is filled with anything, it's the smell of good home cooking—and blood. But not smoke." He swung his chair around and squinted at me. "Five murders in the last week and not a single damned clue—not to mention a squad of men who couldn't find an elephant in a phone booth. And you want to ask me some questions? You're an insurance investigator, huh?"

"Yes," I said.

I was still trying to get a good look at him. There was also something familiar about his voice.

"No damn good," he said. "I never met but one insurance investigator that had any brains at all, and he was a sonuvabitch. A double-dyed, purple-headed sonuvabitch.

Somebody probably killed him a long time ago—out in the fresh air—so there are no more insurance dicks worth anything. What do you want?"

Then I got it. I knew why there was something familiar about him. It made me smile, but the smoke was so thick he couldn't see it.

"Captain Shaffner," I said, "were you in the so-called late war?"

"Of course I was," he said, sounding annoyed. "What's that got to do with it? I thought you were here about insurance."

"There was," I said carefully, "a Lieutenant Shaffner assigned to OSS. He was assigned to a mission behind enemy lines primarily because he'd been a cop before entering the Army. It was a two-man mission and the other man was a sergeant. The mission was successful, but on the way back the lieutenant got trigger-happy like all cops. The sergeant knocked him out, threw him over his shoulder, and carried him back across the lines, and then explained that the lieutenant had been knocked out by concussion from a grenade. ... Of course, you didn't weigh as much then."

He was leaning forward, trying to peer through the swirling smoke. "What did you say your name was?" he asked.

"Milo March."

"You sonuvabitch," he roared. He jumped out of his chair, groped his way across the small office, and grabbed my hand. "You sonuvabitch," he repeated. "Where the hell have you been? You know, I came to in that damned field hospital and never did see you again. Were you the one responsible for me getting that Purple Heart for the so-called concussion?"

"I recommended it," I admitted.

"Caused me more trouble than anything else in my life," he said. "I insisted that nothing of the sort had happened, and they almost turned me over to the nut doctors. Then, when the war was over, my children kept wanting to see the scar from my wound. Hell, I couldn't tell them I got it because some lousy sergeant hit me on the chin."

I laughed. "You earned it—in a way."

"You know," he said, "I tried to have you court-martialed for hitting an officer, but that almost got me a Section Eight, too. It seemed that nobody in the frigging Army ever heard of a Sergeant March."

"Sorry," I told him, "but there was a good reason for that. I was a permanent member of the OSS, and my actual rank then was Captain."

"You sonuvabitch," he said once more. "You know, it probably took me two years to realize that you had saved my life—and your own—that night. I've often thought about it." He chuckled. "As a matter of fact, I used the same tactics on a young detective a few years ago and got a promotion out of it. This calls for a celebration. How about coming out to the house for dinner tonight? Maybe my wife will finally believe the story I told her."

"We'll talk about it later," I said. "I didn't realize that I knew you when I stopped in. I intended to sit here and ask you some questions and hope you'd answer them. Under the circumstances, and since it's about noon, suppose I take you to lunch and we can talk then. If you know a place where we can talk without being overheard."

"That's a great idea," he said. "To hell with the five murders. I know just the place. Let's go."

He struggled into his coat, grabbed a hat, and led the way out of the office. I was grateful for that first breath of fresh air. We went down the corridor and stopped for a second by the desk sergeant.

"Tell Farnsworth to worry about the five murders," the Captain said to the Sergeant. "I'll be back later."

"Yes, sir," the Sergeant said, but he sounded stunned. We left the precinct building and walked for about a block, finally turning in at a little restaurant and bar. There were booths along one wall, and we headed for the farthest one. The owner came from behind the cash register and hurried to meet us.

"It's been a long time, Captain," he said.

Yeah," Captain Shaffner said. "We'll take the last booth, Angelo. Don't put anyone in the booth next to us."

"Of course, Captain," the man said.

We sat down in the booth and the Captain ordered a beer. I had a martini. The Captain looked at me searchingly after we were served our drinks. "So you're back to being an insurance investigator?" he said. "How come you didn't stay in and end up in that fancy-pants CIA?"

"I'd had enough," I said. "But I'm still in the Reserves, and every once in a while they drag me back for a job. There isn't much I can do about that."

"You still look pretty much the same. A little older, maybe, but not much."

"You look much the same, too," I said, "except for about fifty pounds."

"It's that desk job," he said defensively. "The only exercise I get is writing memos and answering memos and yelling at my detectives." He took a long pull at his beer and then looked at me. "What can I do for you, Milo?"

"I'm not sure you can do anything," I said. "I'm only hoping. I'm working for Intercontinental Insurance in New York—on three cases which seem to be related. The first one was in Connecticut. A new invention important to missile control was stolen, and its inventor was either kidnapped or killed."

I stopped to light a cigarette and then went on. "The other two cases were here. One was at Crossen Plastics, where three inventions, all classified by the government, were stolen and two men were killed—accidentally, it says here in small print. The third case was at Santee Chemical. Again, three inventions were stolen. Valuable but not top secret. This time two men committed suicide—according to the official verdict."

We ordered two more drinks and were silent until the waiter brought them and left.

"Much insurance?" the Captain asked.

"At least four million dollars, maybe more."

"How're you making out?"

I smiled. "I'm not working only for the insurance company. I'm supposed to pull a lot of hot chestnuts out of the fire while wearing a blindfold. A very important government man asked me to do what I could to solve their end of the problem—the one that fifty of their men can't. But he wouldn't give me any information, and every time I try to dig up something, I find he's stopped me from getting it. Even in the case of Santee, where nothing was classified, he's blocking me."

"How?"

"Just one example," I said. "This morning I tried to see Mrs. Halsey. Her husband worked for Santee, and all the thefts were strictly industrial. But there was a government man pretending to be a gardener who was there to keep me from seeing her."

"What did you do?"

"Knocked him on his ass, and when he pulled his gun I stepped on his hand and stayed that way until he identified himself. But it didn't get me in to see Mrs. Halsey."

He laughed. "I wish I could have seen that." He brought out a cigar and lit it. "I think I know how you feel, Milo. I worked on the Santee and Crossen cases. I've been a cop all of my life, except for that Army stretch, and I'm now in charge of Homicide, but I've never been treated like such an outsider. Those smart Washington boys did everything but take my badge away from me."

"I don't suppose they told you anything they discovered?"

"Not a word." He puffed on the cigar. "They tried to keep me sitting peacefully at my desk, but I did a little work on my own—while they were busy and after they were finished. I don't know if I found the same things they did. They didn't tell me what they found, and I didn't tell them what I found. Seemed fair that way." He chuckled.

"Do you mind giving me some information?" I asked.

"Well, I guess I wouldn't normally say anything—at least, not right away. I have an idea that the government men wouldn't like it. But I owe you something for that Purple Heart. I don't know anything about the thefts themselves, but I know a little about what happened afterward, maybe even a few things they don't know in Washington. I'll answer any questions you want to ask, but do me one favor."

"What?"

"Forget where you heard the answers."

"It's a deal," I said. "Let me guess part of it. Sometime before there were any thefts, a strange man showed up here. He ran ads in the newspapers for chemical and plastics engineers. They were phrased to appeal to just such men as the two at Santee and the two at Crossen. His name was C. Jackson."

"Right about everything except the name. He called himself Carl Johnson. He took a suite in a hotel and ran the ads. A lot of men answered, but he only saw four. Robert Halsey, Dan Frame, Richard Matson, and Carl Kelly. Shortly after that Mr. Johnson gave up his suite, and he and his friend left."

"His friend?"

"Yes. She called herself Ann Brent, but I don't think that was her real name. She stayed at another hotel, and there was never any obvious connection between them. I discovered it by accident."

"What address did Johnson give when he registered?"

"The Johnson Personnel Agency in New York. The girl gave the same address. But she wasn't with him when he came back."

That surprised me. "He came back?"

He nodded. "Just about the time the first of the four men died. Only he called himself Calvin Johns and stayed at a different hotel."

"How did you find that out?"

"One of the bellhops at the hotel where he first stayed had quit his job and gone to work in this other hotel. He recognized Johns as Johnson and mentioned it to one of my men. The girl wasn't with him that second time—but there was a man with him."

"Who?"

"Called himself Joe Pitcher, but I'll bet it was a phony. He was a little weasel of a guy and spoke with some kind of accent. I went after them when the second hit-and-run happened, but they had already checked out. I sent through a wanted on them to the New York police—they couldn't find them either."

"Tell me about the hit-and-run accidents," I said.

"No accidents," he said. "The same car hit both men. Identical paint was found on the clothes of both men. Two weeks later we found the car. It had been stolen in Harrisburg. There were threads on the front of the car that came from the suits the two men were wearing at the times they were hit. I don't suppose I have to tell you that there were no fingerprints, or other evidence, in the car."

"The government know about this?"

"I don't think so," he said. There was a note of satisfaction in his voice. "As I said, they didn't tell me anything, so I didn't tell them anything."

I motioned for two more drinks and waited until they were served. "Any ideas why Matson and Kelly stole those processes for Jackson? They both made good money and had bright futures with the company."

"Plenty of ideas. Jackson, or Johnson, operated in two ways. He had plenty of money to spend and he also used blackmail. Matson and Kelly were easy for him. Matson liked horses, although nobody in the company and none of his friends knew about it. He'd been winning for several months and then he started taking a beating. I know that he lost thirty thousand dollars just before the thefts, and he may have lost more. He made good money, but not good enough to stand up under that. He owed ten thousand and he couldn't pay it off without taking a mortgage on his home or borrowing. Either one would have revealed his secret. He paid off the ten thousand just about the time the thefts occurred."

"How do you know this?"

"From his bookie. He provides us with considerable information in return for not being bothered too much by the vice squad. He came in with the information as soon as Matson was killed."

"The CIA know about this?"

"I don't think so."

"What about Kelly?"

He smiled. "He did a stretch in Ohio when he was just a kid. This Jackson found out about it and used it."

"How the hell did he get clearance to work on classified material?"

"His family were big shots, and they managed to get the records removed. He apparently went straight after he got out."

"What did he go up for?"

"Grand larceny. He served the minimum, then was paroled."

"If the records were removed, how did you find out about it? How did Jackson find out about it?"

"It happened in Cleveland. I have an old friend on the force there. The cop who arrested Kelly retired just about the time the kid got out. He bought himself a home in Cleveland Heights that cost more than any cop could afford. He's an old man now, but he suddenly got prosperous again shortly before Jackson showed up here."

"But there must have been others who knew about it?"

"Sure. The judge died while the kid was in prison. The warden at the prison retired and has since died. The prison records on Kelly retired when the warden did. The library files of the newspapers are mysteriously missing the issues that covered his arrest and trial. I told you his family were important people. Even the transcript of the trial has vanished."

"It's nice to be important," I said dryly. "What about Halsey and Frame? Your official verdict was that they committed suicide."

"Sure," he said. He bit savagely on the cigar. "I was told to say that—by a nice, gentle man from Washington. I'm not sure that I wouldn't have done so anyway, since I couldn't get my hands on the man who was responsible. Actually, I think one of them was a suicide, but I'd swear that the other one wasn't. And the one that was wouldn't have been if that Jackson had never showed up."

"I'm listening," I said.

"They didn't work on security jobs, so they were never checked out very closely before or after. I worked real hard on them because it didn't smell right. You know what I mean?"

"I know the smell," I said. "It's all over these cases."

"Do you know anything about the suicides?" he asked abruptly.

"Not a damn thing. Everyone's reluctant to even admit that I exist."

"Halsey hanged himself in his garage," he said gravely. "He climbed on a box, tied the rope over a rafter and around his neck, and kicked the box out from under his feet. I think that was legitimate."

"Why?"

He took a deep breath. "Halsey was a homosexual, at least before the time he met his wife. It took me a long time to dig that up. He lived in New York and met Betty Allen when he was on a visit here. My information is that he has slipped a couple of times since then on visits to New York, but the last time was more than a year ago. I think he was pretty much straightened out, but Jackson must have dug it up some way and used it against him. I guess he couldn't take the idea that it might come out. I don't think I would like it if this became part of any record."

"It won't as far as I'm concerned," I said.

He nodded. "I didn't think it would or I wouldn't have mentioned it."

"What about Frame?" I asked.

"I got that pretty well pinned down, too. Dan Frame was a local boy. Smart as a whip. Never made a wrong move in his life until just before the thefts at Santee."

"He slipped?" I asked.

"I guess you could call it that. Somebody—and my guess

is it was that Jackson—got him drunk and teamed him up with Ann Brent. Anyway, he checked into a motel with her and spent the night. It took me about a week to discover that. I don't think anyone else knows it—except Ann Brent and Jackson. But that must have been the lever to get him to cooperate. It probably was almost too much for him to face, but Dan Frame never committed suicide. That boy was a fighter."

"So what happened?"

"The record shows that Dan Frame drove his car about two miles beyond the city limits, parked, and then blew his brains out with his own gun. Nonsense. It was Dan's gun, all right. But there were no fingerprints on the steering wheel of his car—and his should have been on it. There were also no fingerprints on the gun with which he supposedly shot himself. In addition, I ran a nitrate test on Dan's hands, and he had not fired a gun."

"Sounds pretty convincing," I said.

"There's one more thing," he said. "Dan Frame had pulled his car off the highway into a little grove. And that is where he supposedly killed himself. But our investigation proved that another car had pulled in behind him and had then turned around and left. We have casts of the tire treads, but we haven't been able to pin them to any specific car."

"This is all part of the record?" I asked.

He hesitated. "No. Not the official file. I have it in a personal file. If I can use it to convict a murderer, it'll become a part of the official record. In the meantime, it's not going to be something available to newspapermen—or even the CIA or the FBI. I know it's not living up to the traditions of my office, but that's the way it is. If I could—or can—convict the murderer, then I will use all of it. But until then I'm not going to hurt innocent people just to get some publicity for myself. Take it or leave it."

"I'll take it," I said. "I even agree with you. In fact, I'm sure that the murderer is well out of your jurisdiction and the jurisdiction of everyone else here—except me."

He smiled around the cigar. "That's why I told you. I thought that a sergeant who would clobber his lieutenant, then carry him across five miles of enemy lines and recommend him for the Purple Heart, might forget some of the rules that the rest of us live by. You will, won't you, Milo?"

"If I can," I said.

"Whoever he is," the Captain said, "he's probably somewhere in Europe. It won't be easy with international law involved."

"I'm sure it won't," I said. I reached for a cigarette and made a point of pushing my coat far enough so that he could see the gun in my shoulder holster. "But I'll try to find a way to solve the cases."

He chuckled. "Maybe that night twenty years ago was lucky for both of us. You don't know it, Milo, but I'm a pretty good cop. I don't like to see people unduly hurt and I don't like to be told—even by the government—to keep my mouth shut. As you mentioned, I've grown a little fat and I guess I'm more concerned about security than I should be. In fact, in all honesty, I probably told you everything I know in hopes that you would act for both of us. Then maybe I can finish out another two years and retire with my pension, a good conscience—and my Purple Heart."

"I hope so," I said. "But I'll level with you. Maybe I owe you something for clipping you in the jaw twenty years ago, but my knuckles don't even hurt now. I have a job to do. I don't get any pension, but I get paid very well for the work I do. I expect to deliver full value for it. And without sentiment. It's sentiment that kills people like us."

"I think you're right," he said sadly. "Shall we have some lunch? It may kill us, too."

So we had lunch. It wasn't great and it wasn't bad. We finished it off with brandy, toasting World War II. I don't really go for that jazz, but I've discovered that the guys who griped the most while it was going on are the ones with the fondest memories, so I go along.

"Now," the Captain said, as we were leaving, "how about coming out to the house for dinner tonight?"

"I think I'd better take a rain check," I said. "I won't find our Mr. Jackson at a dinner table. I promise you that I'll come back for the dinner when this is over. Okay?"

"Okay," he said.

I left him in front of the precinct and got in my car, heading back for New York. I got the idea in the first ten blocks, so I tried a few experiments. By the time I reached the turnpike, I was certain. Somebody in a new Pontiac was following me.

FIVE

Driving just below the turnpike speed limit, I kept a close watch on the Pontiac in my rearview mirror. It stayed an even distance behind me, close enough so that I couldn't suddenly swerve off at an exit and lose it. There was only one person in it, but the car was never near enough for me to get a good look at him.

I was pretty certain it wasn't a government agent. They had so many men covering all points that they didn't have to follow me. I could be sure there would be an agent lurking around wherever I stopped to ask questions. So who was following me? Maybe I'd been wrong in assuming that Jackson and his friends had long since departed.

I turned north when I reached the New Jersey turnpike, and then it wasn't too long until I reached New York. The Pontiac was still remaining faithful to me. I didn't try to lose him even after I got into New York City. I drove up to Greenwich Village and parked on Barrow Street near one of my favorite restaurants. I noticed that the Pontiac pulled to the curb about fifty yards back of me. I locked the car and walked across to the restaurant.

It was near the cocktail hour and there were several people at the bar, but the section near the door was empty. The bartender gave me a smile and started to reach for a bottle of gin.

"Not just yet, Al," I said. "I'm going to the men's room. I think a man is going to follow me in very soon. Unless he sits up here by himself, I want you to indicate which one he is when I come out. Okay?"

He nodded and I went on back to the men's room. I smoked a cigarette and waited about five minutes. Then I went out. There was a man sitting at the end of the bar, and the bartender was just placing a whiskey and soda in front of him. He was a small, thin-faced man who reminded me of the description Captain Shaffner had given of Jackson's companion.

He ignored me as I sat down a couple of stools away from him. Al mixed me a martini and put it in front of me. He winked as he placed the glass on the bar. I drank the martini slowly.

"Well," I said to Al when I had finished, "I guess I'll go home. Maybe I'll see you later."

I walked out without looking at the little man. When I reached the sidewalk, I turned to the left instead of heading for my car. I walked slowly. I hadn't gone far before I heard the sound of the restaurant door opening and closing. I didn't look around.

There was a large apartment building next to the restaurant. It was in two sections, one with an entrance on Barrow Street and one with an entrance on the next block. In between, there was a large, fairly dark court. There was a shortcut into the court just beyond the restaurant where narrow, steep steps went down from the street. That's the way I went.

When I reached the court, I stepped to one side into the shadows and waited. A moment later I heard him coming down the steps. He was moving carefully and trying to be quiet, but the stairs were dark and I could hear the scrape of leather against concrete as he felt for his footing.

He reached the bottom of the stairs, took a step into the court, and stopped. He was in a half crouch, looking around to see where I'd gone. The faint light glinted on something in his hand, and I was sure it was a gun. He was within two feet of where I stood. I carefully eased my own gun out of the holster and waited until he looked the other way. I took one step forward and brought the barrel of my gun down on the back of his head. He slumped to the concrete, the gun clattering from his hand.

I bent down and felt his pulse. It was steady, but he'd be out for a while. I felt through his coat and found his wallet. It was too dark there to see anything, so I took it with me and went back up the steps to the street. I stopped on the sidewalk and looked through the wallet. There was a thick wad of money and a driver's license in the name of Joseph Pitcher. That was the name that Captain Shaffner had mentioned.

There was a liquor store nearby. I went in and bought a half pint of whiskey. Then I went back to the court. He was still lying in the same position. I used my foot to push the gun nearer to him. I opened the whiskey bottle and poured most of the contents over him. I used my handkerchief to take my prints off it, pressed it into his hand, and left it there. I replaced his wallet and went back upstairs. I found a public phone booth and called the police. I told them there was a troublesome drunk in the courtyard of the apartment building and hung up before they could ask my name.

I went back to my car and drove off. As I turned into Hudson, I saw a prowl car on its way down Barrow, so they'd probably get there before he recovered.

I parked in front of my apartment on Perry Street, picked up my mail, and went upstairs. The first thing I did was call Western Union and send a telegram to Captain Shaffner. I told him that he'd probably find Pitcher in the custody of the Sixth Precinct on charges of drunkenness and carrying a deadly weapon.

After I'd taken care of that, I took a shower, shaved, and got dressed. I went out and had two very dry martinis and an excellent dinner at a little place around the corner. I picked up a couple of papers and went back home. I'd done enough work for one day.

Back in my apartment, I undressed, poured a V.O. on the rocks, and stretched out on the bed. I sipped on the drink and thought about the case.

It was already clear that I was going to have to dig up anything I got all by myself. If anything, I would run into opposition and not cooperation. I was looking for a man who, although he undoubtedly had an organization of some sort, was still an individual operator. My guess was that while politics was certainly involved, especially with those items that were classified, he was primarily interested in money. I was certain that he was no longer in the United States. The question was: where was he at the moment?

The answer couldn't be easy. If it were, the CIA would have already discovered it and the General wouldn't have been asking for my help. I didn't have a very good description of

Jackson, or whatever his name was, but I was beginning to get a good idea of what he was. He was a very good operator, willing to work long, hard hours to achieve what he wanted. He was also completely ruthless and would stop at nothing. If I could believe Captain Shaffner—and I was sure I could— he had been responsible for the death of at least four men, perhaps five.

I doubted if he had a large organization. He didn't sound like the sort of man who would trust many people even when he was paying for their loyalty. Pitcher, for example. Jackson must have still been paying him to watch what was going on, but he was probably the only one left behind. He had probably kept a close watch on everything and knew the government agents hadn't gotten a hot lead. He must have known about Shaffner's work and had begun to worry about me after my meeting with the Captain.

Well, I thought, Shaffner would probably keep him out of circulation for a while. If not, then the New York police would, on the charge of possession of a gun. I made another drink, read the newspapers, and went to sleep.

I was up early the next morning. I cooked some bacon and eggs and had three cups of coffee. Then I was ready for a new day. I drove across town and parked near the building that Jackson, or Johnson, had given as his address. As I expected, none of his companies were listed on the board. I went looking for the custodian; the rents were high enough for him to be called that rather than a mere janitor. He was in the basement. His name was Swenson. He was a big, hairy man, about sixty years old, with a mustache that looked as if it had been run through a ringer. I told him who I was and said that I'd like to ask him a few questions. He was agreeable.

"A few months ago," I said, "you had a tenant here known as the Jackson Professional Services?"

"Yes," he said.

"What can you tell me about them?" I asked.

He stuffed tobacco into his pipe and lit it. "Wasn't no them," he said, "just Mr. Jackson. A nice fellow. But he didn't have much business and I guess he just couldn't make it. Was only here a few months and then moved out. Don't know where he went."

"How long was he here?"

"Maybe three months. He didn't have any business and he gave up all of his offices."

"He had more than one?"

"Three."

"All under the same name?"

"No. He had Jackson Professional Services, Johnson Personnel, and the Calvin Johns Company. But they were all his companies and he paid the rent."

"Did he have any employees?"

"A girl. A very pretty girl. Blond and pretty and young. Swedish. Miss Brent."

"She was the only one?"

"Yes."

"Did he pay the rent to you?"

"No. I only take care of the building. The rent he paid to Mr. Ackerman."

"Who's he?"

"The manager. He has an office on the tenth floor. But he was a nice gentleman and Miss Brent was a nice lady."

"I'm sure," I said gently. "Did he have much business?"

"I don't think so."

"What was his business?" I asked.

"He was trying to get jobs for people. It was a good thing he was trying to do."

"Was he an American?"

"I don't think so," he said slowly. "Maybe English."

"And Miss Brent?" He hesitated. "I'm not sure," he said. "She spoke English very well, but I think maybe she was Swedish, Norwegian, or Danish—there was something in her voice. I cannot explain it."

"I know what you mean," I said. "Thanks. I'll see Mr. Ackerman."

He nodded, puffing on his pipe, and I left. I took the elevator to the tenth floor. Mr. Ackerman was in. He looked like a hundred other real estate managers—thin and hungry. I showed him my identification and he got nervous.

"I want to ask you about one of your former tenants," I told him.

He relaxed. "Who?"

"Chris Jackson. Jackson Professional Services. Johnson Personnel and the Calvin Johns Company."

He looked even more relieved. "He was here only about three months. Had three offices. I guess it didn't work out for him and he left. No forwarding address." He considered it for a minute. "Others have been asking for him—including the police."

"I know," I said. "You saw Mr. Jackson yourself?"

"Many times."

"Could you describe him?"

He frowned. "He was a bit on the heavy side. I would say a hundred and eighty pounds, maybe five feet eight. Dark hair. Pinkish sort of face. I would guess forty to forty-five years old. What is this about, Mr. March?"

"Insurance," I said. "Did he pay his rent by check or with cash?"

"Check. And they were always good."

"Would you mind," I asked, "telling me the name of the bank on which the checks were drawn?"

"Of course not," he said with dignity. "We always try to cooperate. They were drawn on the Sterling National Bank here in New York. It is one of our better banks."

"I'm sure it is," I said gravely. "Thank you, Mr. Ackerman. I shall make a note of your cooperation." With that pleasant exchange, I left.

I made a call to Martin Raymond at Intercontinental and learned that they held a lot of stock in Sterling National. Things like that always helped. I hung up and headed for the nearest branch of the bank. After some small talk I finally ended up with a vice-president named Minor. It fitted him perfectly. I identified myself and sat down, giving him my executive smile.

"What can I do for you, Mr. March?" he asked. He sounded nervous. Bankers always sound nervous when they know they're going to be asked questions by someone connected with stockholders. They are only secure when they are asking the questions.

"I'd like a little information," I said politely. Bankers also like it if you're polite. "A few months ago you had a depositor named C. Jackson—although the account may have been under the name of Jackson Professional Services or Johnson Personnel or the Calvin Jones Company, or all four."

"Just a minute," he said. He scurried off to the records and came back a few minutes later with several folders.

"Mr. Jackson did do business with us," he said, "but you understand that these records are confidential."

"Of course," I said. I decided it was time to stop being polite. "However, since Intercontinental is a major stockholder in this bank and since I represent Intercontinental, I have a feeling that they might take a dim view of any lack of cooperation. If you doubt my word, I suggest that you phone Mr. Raymond at Intercontinental. I think he will straighten you out."

"No, no, you misunderstood me, Mr. March," he said hastily. "What is it you would like to know?"

"Just one thing," I said. "I presume that Mr. Jackson must have made deposits in his account or accounts. I want to know where that money came from."

He shuffled through the folders as though he expected a snake to strike from between two sheets of paper. Finally he looked up. "Mr. Jackson," he said, "received money from two sources. All of his deposits were in the form of bank drafts. They came from Switzerland and Sweden. The drafts were made out to be deposited to his account. Mr. Jackson maintained three accounts here, and some of the monies were transferred from his personal account to his business accounts."

"The drafts that came from Switzerland," I asked, "might have come from a numbered account?"

"It's possible," he said cautiously, "although I cannot say. The draft would not show that. We are aware that there are many persons with numbered accounts there and that they can transfer money anywhere by means of a bank draft."

"What about the money from Sweden?"

He consulted his records again. "That also came in the form of bank drafts, but there is an indication that the money came from a commercial account there." He hesitated, then plunged ahead. "As a matter of fact, it is indicated that the money from Sweden was drawn from the account of Jason Aktiebolag* in Stockholm."

"The checks were always good?"

He drew himself up with dignity. "They were bank drafts. Banks do not write bad checks."

"No?" I said gently. "What about the banks that failed? I seem to remember five or six that failed in this country in the past few months. I would have hated to get one of their bank drafts the day after they folded."

I left him sitting there with a stunned look on his face. The next step was nothing but legwork. I drove downtown to Centre Street and stopped in to see a cop I knew—Lieutenant Johnny Rockland. He looked at me sourly as I walked into his office.

"Don't tell me," he said. "Let me guess. You had some time off and you drifted downtown to visit with your old friend Johnny. You don't want anything; it's entirely social."

---

* After Swedish company names, *Aktiebolag* is the equivalent of *Limited* (Ltd.).

"Partly right," I said. "The other part is that I want to do you a favor."

"Your favors I can do without," he said. "What do you want, Milo?"

"Me?" I said in mock surprise. "I don't want anything. I've become a psychic. I'll even make you a bet."

"What kind of bet?"

"About three months ago, somewhere between here and Thirty-fifth Street, probably on the East Side, the police found an abandoned panel truck. It may or may not have had lettering on it. If there was lettering, it was *Peerless Laundry*. The truck was probably stolen and may have had other lettering on it before that. There were no fingerprints anywhere on it. There may have been two empty laundry bags in the rear of the truck. The case was never solved."

I leaned back and lit a cigarette.

"Why did I ever meet you?" he asked in resignation. He picked up the phone and made a call. He asked a number of questions and then hung up. He looked at me with disgust. "I don't know whether you're psychic or psychotic," he said, "but a panel truck was picked up on Twenty-seventh Street just about that time. It was painted black, but under that there was a coat of white paint and it had the name of Peerless Laundry on it. Under that was another coat of white paint and another name. There were no fingerprints and there were two empty laundry bags in the back. The lab reported that there had been someone in each bag. There were threads from suits and a few short hairs. The truck had been stolen a month earlier. Now, what's your story?"

"I don't know," I said.

He threw up his hands. "Another fishing expedition. I should have known it."

"No, Johnny," I said. "A fishing expedition, yes. But not with you. It has to do with theft, murder, and the possession of classified government property. In addition, I'm positive that the guilty party is no longer within your jurisdiction. Even if he were, the Federal boys would probably get first crack at him."

"That's all you can tell me?" he asked.

"That's all," I said. "In fact, Johnny, it's so damned secret that nobody will tell *me* anything. And there's something like fifty CIA men breathing down my neck to make sure that I don't learn something I shouldn't know."

"All right," he said. "In the meantime, I'm a public servant and I'm supposed to earn my small salary. Drop in the next time you feel lonely."

"Thanks, Johnny," I said. "Kiss the wife and kids for me."

"And poison them?" he said. "On your way, you imitation cop."

"I'm a taxpayer," I said. "You should be more respectful." I left before he could think of an answer.

I got into my car, drove over to Broadway, and started uptown. I had gone only a few blocks when I realized I was being followed again. From the looks of the car, I guessed this was an agent. I didn't like it. It took me about fifteen blocks to lose him, but I finally managed it. Then I headed happily for Kennedy Airport.

I struck pay dirt at the sixth airlines desk. It took them a little time, but I finally learned that at about the right date, a Jason Johansson had taken the flight to Stockholm, Sweden. He had bought two tickets. That sounded right. This Johansson had used the name of Johnson in New York City and in Philadelphia, and he'd received money from a man named Jason in Sweden. I made a reservation and drove back into the city.

When I reached Perry Street I saw that my apartment was staked out. There was a car parked across the street that looked like the one that had followed me from Centre Street. The man behind the wheel was being much too interested in his newspaper, so I was sure of what it was. I parked behind him and went across to my apartment.

It had been a warm morning, so I took a quick shower. Without bothering to get dressed, I poured myself a drink and sat down. After a couple of sips, I reached for the telephone. I stopped just as my hand touched it. I had a sudden thought. The government agents were paying so much attention to me, it was very possible that they had also tapped my phone. If they had my apartment staked out, they certainly wouldn't overlook my phone. I took my hand away as if I'd been about to touch a hot stove.

I finished my drink and poured another one while I thought about the problem. Then I made some lunch and had a cup of coffee with it. I walked over to the window and peered through the blinds. The car was still parked across the street. The driver had the newspaper propped up against the steering wheel, but he wasn't paying much attention to it.

I set my alarm clock to go off in two hours and went to sleep. That would give me plenty of time.

The alarm went off on time and I got up. I shaved and packed my clothes. I decided to have a little fun before I left. I picked up the phone and dialed Meridian 7-1212. The operator gave me the correct time. When it was over, I spoke: "Be sure to set your watches, boys. Washington likes you to be accurate." I hung up.

Downstairs, I crossed the street, ignoring the man in the car, and placed my luggage in my car. Then, bending over so he wouldn't see me, I moved over to the car ahead of me. I quickly removed the core from the valve of the tire and tossed it back down the street. The tire was half flat before the driver heard the sound of the escaping air.

Suddenly he became aware of it and opened the door to look back. I was standing there, admiring the deflation of the tire.

"What the hell's going on?" he demanded.

"I was just about to tell you," I said sweetly. "It looks as if you're getting a flat tire. Must have picked up a nail."

"While I was parked here?" he demanded angrily.

"Probably a cheap tire," I said cheerfully. "You know how it is with those. I think you'll find a service station about three blocks from here. Or there's a public phone about a block away and you can call the Auto Club. Tough luck, old chap."

I climbed into my car and drove off while he stood there, glaring at me in impotent rage. It brightened up my whole day.

I took the car back to the rental agency and then hailed a cab and gave the driver the address of Intercontinental. I checked the street when he stopped in front of the building, but it didn't look as if they had it staked out. Still, the General knew I worked for Intercontinental, and I would have given odds that he had a tap on their phones, too. I paid off the driver and went upstairs.

The usual receptionist was at the desk, with her usual plunging neckline. I looked down while she looked up.

"Hello, Mr. March," she said. For her, that was a brilliant opening. "You want to see Mr. Raymond?" She started to reach for the phone.

"Don't phone," I said quickly. "Here's what I want you to do, honey. Get up and walk back to Raymond's secretary. Tell her to have him meet me immediately in the doctor's office. No phone calls."

She looked doubtful.

"It's okay, honey," I said. "I'll stay here and see that no one takes the carpeting while you're gone—although there's nothing here that anyone would want to steal when you're not present."

"Oh, you!" she exclaimed. It was one of her better answers. But she got up and marched back toward the executive wing. I watched her go and was glad that she didn't wear a girdle. There is much to be said for the simple life.

She was back in less than five minutes—and she looked just as great coming as she did going. "Mr. Raymond will be right there, Mr. March," she said, as she sat down behind the desk. The way she did it was an art.

"Honey," I said, "I wish they would make you a vice-president so that I could have these secret meetings with you. Corporations just aren't run the way they should be. I'll be seeing you—I hope." I turned the other way and entered the wing where the common people worked. I walked through what was known as the bullpen, filled with salesmen and investigators, and went into the doctor's office.

"You!" he said when he saw me. "I'm not giving any vitamin B shots for a hangover, so take your business somewhere else. I'll give you a couple of aspirin if you want them."

"That's what I like," I said. "Intercontinental is just one big happy family. Everybody loves everybody else—but there is only one executive vice-president and he's going to be here any minute. In the meantime, when did I have my last smallpox vaccination?"

"How the hell do I know?" he asked. He walked over to his files and thumbed through them. "A year ago."

"So it's still good?"

"Yes."

The door opened and Martin Raymond entered. He glared at me. "What the hell is this Boy Scout stuff?" he demanded.

"Personally," I said, "I prefer Girl Scouts. Graduated."

"I mean what the hell's the idea of bringing me over here?"

"Did it ever occur to you that your phone might be tapped?"

That stopped him for a minute. "They wouldn't dare," he said finally, but he didn't believe it himself.

"Stop kidding yourself," I told him. "I've had CIA men breathing down my neck from the beginning of this case. When I try to see someone, there's a CIA man there saying that I shouldn't. My apartment is staked out. I am being followed. And, believe me, Martin, old boy, this is not meant to be cooperation. They are not going to give any help at all, and they are hoping that I will solve everything for them without any information. I might as well be rolling dice."

"All right," he said with a sigh, "what's this about?"

"I think I have spotted our chief villain. I think he went to Sweden shortly after he pulled off his little tricks. I am going to follow him tonight. I need money."

"You always need money," he said sourly. "Martinis cost more money in Sweden?"

"I don't think it's going to end there," I said. "Besides, they have a new thing which you may not have heard about. It's called flying. Of course, if you'd rather that I took a sloop or maybe just quit the case, just say so."

"All right, all right," he said angrily. "How much does the CIA know?"

"Almost nothing," I said. "If they did, they wouldn't be dogging me so much. Also, I had some luck. Make up your so-called mind."

"How much do you need?"

"I still have money left from what you gave me, but you'd better let me have some more. I don't know where the hell I go after I get to Sweden. It's much easier to get money out of you face to face than by cablegram."

"How much?" he repeated.

"Better give me two thousand," I said. "You know I'll account for every penny of it."

"Sure," he said. "You'll put down 'refreshments'—meaning martinis—and 'entertainment'—meaning broads. What the hell am I supposed to tell the Board of Directors?"

"Tell them that I got drunk and shacked up with a broad," I suggested brightly.

"Bah!" he said.

"You might also ask them," I said, "whether they want to save four or five million dollars or if they want to believe that life is full of soft drinks, honest people, and characters who can't tell the difference between a man and a woman. If they do, you'd better order glasses for all of them at company expense. You'll save money in the long run. And, believe me, buster, it is a long run."

He sighed heavily. "All right. Wait here and I'll have my secretary bring you the money. But you'd better deliver—or I'll have you hung and quartered."

"Make it halved," I said. "I look better in profile."

He grunted and left.

The doctor looked at me. "You're a thief," he said. "Two thousand dollars! How do you get away with that?"

"Natural charm," I said. I smiled at him. "The trouble with you, Doctor, is you've spent most of your life examining the piles of desk workers. It gives you a backward view of life."

"This is a fine business," he said with dignity. "It's people like you who ruin it."

"Ruin, hell," I said. "Wrecked 'em."

He stared at me for a minute, then laughed. "I have to hand it to you, Milo. I've been in this business for twenty-five years, and you're the most arrogant bastard I've ever seen in it. They ought to make you the chairman of the board."

"Don't try to work your wiles on me," I told him. "I'll let you give me a shot, but you won't catch me bending over in your examining room. The first thing I'd know you'd have both hands on my shoulders."

He leaned back and laughed until the tears came into his eyes. "The insurance business," he said finally, "is the biggest con business in the world, and you are the biggest con artist in it."

It seemed to me that it was more dignified to ignore this than to answer it, and I was helped in the decision by the arrival of Martin Raymond's secretary. She handed me a bulging envelope.

"I don't know what you found out, buster," she said, "but it must be a pip. The last time anyone handed out company money like this was the year that Lincoln ran for president. What's the secret?"

"About five million dollars," I said. "It doesn't mean any more to Mr. Martin Raymond than two gallons of his own blood." I took the money from the envelope, counted it, and stuck it in my pocket. "If you wage slaves will excuse me, I'm off into the wild blue yonder." I gave them my best smile and left.

I took another taxi to the airport. It was soon time to get on the plane. I went through the gate and climbed aboard. I was staring out the window when the plane started to roll down the runway. There was a man standing at the gate waving his arms angrily. I realized there was something familiar about him. Then I knew what it was. He was the man who had been parked in front of my apartment.

I laughed, and as soon as we were up in the air I told the stewardess to bring me a martini. It tasted better than anything I'd had in a long time.

SIX

The plane came down in Copenhagen. I had to change planes, and there would be a wait of several hours before another plane left for Stockholm. I made sure of the time and wandered out into the city. I stopped in a restaurant and had a *smorrebrod*, an open-faced sandwich heaped with vegetables and seafood, and a cold bottle of Danish beer.

Copenhagen is a beautiful town. After I left the restaurant, I walked around the city and enjoyed it. When it was time to get back to the airport I hailed a taxi. It was a short flight from Copenhagen and then we came down in Stockholm, another beautiful city. I checked through the customs and took a taxi to a hotel.

I had already decided that I wouldn't try to do any work until the next day. I did, however, glance through the telephone book. Jason Aktiebolag was listed. I wrote down the address. I changed clothes and ordered a drink and a newspaper to be sent up to my room. I wouldn't say that I was an expert in Swedish, but I could read enough of it to get most of the news out of the paper. And I was able to catch up with the latest adventures of Stor-Klas and Lill-Klas—better known in America as Mutt and Jeff—and Micky Mus.

I also learned that Lux soap *är verkligen ett underbart diskmedel!* I could have learned that in New York. And I noticed that Swedish cats were very fond of something called Kit-E-Kat *färdig kattmat*. It was quite educational.

When I had finished reading about the food delights in store for cats, I went downstairs and explored the conveniences of the hotel. There was a very fine bar, where I had a couple more drinks, and then I went on to the dining room. The food was excellent. Afterwards I took a walk around the city, stopping three or four times to explore other bars. I returned to the hotel and went to bed early.

The next morning I had breakfast in the hotel and took a taxi to Jason Aktiebolag. I was shown into the office of a Mr. Nilsson, who apparently was the general manager. I introduced myself as an American businessman who was interested in surveying Swedish industry. To my relief, Mr. Nilsson spoke English. He was also quite friendly and willing to devote time to my questions.

"I understand," I said, "that you deal in plastics?"

"That is true," he said, "although that is not our entire business. We do manufacture many plastic items for sale throughout Europe. In addition to that, we deal in various patents which we lease to manufacturers all over Europe."

"Do you develop your own patents?"

"Many of them, yes. Others we buy, usually on a royalty basis."

"Who is the owner of your company?"

"Herr Jason Johansson is the president and the largest stockholder."

"Would it be possible for me to make an appointment with him?"

"I'm afraid not at the moment," he said. "Herr Johansson is traveling through Europe, calling on our customers."

"Where is he now?"

"I don't know where he is today," he said with a smile. "Herr Johansson has complete confidence in his staff here, and he seldom gets in touch with us while he is traveling. But orders do come in as a result of his work."

"You have no idea where he is now?"

"No. He may be in West Germany or Holland or France. I don't really know."

"When will he be back?"

"I couldn't say. Sometimes he lets us know a few hours or a day ahead of time, and sometimes he just appears."

"Well, that's one way of keeping you on your toes," I said dryly. "Does he also travel to America?"

"Occasionally, yes."

"When was the last time he was there?"

For the first time he hesitated. "I am not sure. I believe it was perhaps a year ago. Herr Johansson is a genius; he is not like other men. He goes and comes as he pleases; he may notify us or he may not. He buys and sells to suit himself, but always he makes a profit."

"I'm sure he does," I said. "Well, thank you, Mr. Nilsson. It's been most educational. Does Mr. Johansson maintain a home in Stockholm?"

"Oh, yes. He has a very nice home out on the edge of the city. It is unfortunate that he cannot spend more time there."

"I'm sure it is. His wife must find it hard to have him gone so much."

He permitted himself another smile. "Herr Johansson is a confirmed bachelor.

Perhaps it is just as well. A woman would find it most difficult to have a husband who is never home."

"But then there are girlfriends."

He spread his hands wide. "I would assume so, but one does not ask one's employer about such things."

"Of course not," I agreed gravely. "Do you happen to have a photograph of him around—so that I will recognize him if I happen to run into him? I travel a good deal myself."

"Unfortunately, no. Herr Johansson does not like to have his photograph taken. Some people are like that."

"I've noticed," I said. "Thank you again, Mr. Nilsson. I'm sorry I took up so much of your time."

"I was happy to oblige," he said, but he didn't sound as if he meant it. "Please feel free to visit us at any time. If Herr Johansson returns, I will tell him that you called."

"You do that," I said. I got up and left.

My next stop was the bank which had sent drafts to Jackson, or Johnson, or Johansson, in New York. I was finally shown into the office of our equivalent of a vice-president. Since Intercontinental had a branch office in Sweden, I was treated with a certain amount of respect once I had identified myself.

"What can I do for you, Herr March?" the man asked. His name was Lindquist.

"I am interested in Jason Johansson of Jason Aktiebolag. I understand that he does business with you."

"Yes. Herr Johansson and his company both have substantial accounts here. Of course, you understand, it is not possible to reveal details about these accounts."

"Of course," I said. "As a matter of fact, I am not interested in how much money he has. I believe that he was in America a few months ago and that you sent several bank drafts to his account in an American bank?"

"That is true," he admitted.

"Could you tell me where Mr. Johansson is at the moment?"

He shook his head. "We have not heard from him. When he returned from America, he was in here to go over his accounts and to draw some money. He also arranged for us to send money to New York City in America. We have not heard from him since, although he did say he was going to several countries on the Continent."

"Who did he send money to in America?"

He paused for a second before answering. "I see nothing wrong with telling you that. It was to a Herr Joseph Pitcher. Herr Johansson said it was a business matter."

"It certainly was," I said. "Tell me, Mr. Lindquist, do you happen to know Mr. Johansson socially as well as in a business way?"

"Not exactly," he said. "I believe that I have seen him socially perhaps four times since he has been doing business with the bank. You must understand that Herr Johansson spends much of his time out of the country on business trips. Even when he is here, he does not go out much."

"He must have personal interests or hobbies."

"Not really." He shook his head. "Herr Johansson is one of those men who devote almost their entire time to business. It is a successful way to operate, but I should imagine a lonely way to live."

"You said almost?" I asked.

"Yes. I know that Herr Johansson is very fond of good food and also enjoys the company of beautiful women when he is not working. I believe he has no other interests."

"He has a mistress?"

"Perhaps. I do not know."

"Does he have a favorite restaurant here in Stockholm?"

"Yes. I believe he usually goes to Askling's when he is here. I saw him there a couple of times, and I know that he often spoke of it."

"Thank you, Mr. Lindquist," I said. "I appreciate your help and will certainly include that in my report to my company."

"That is very kind of you, Herr March. We consider Intercontinental one of our best overseas customers." He hesitated, then plunged ahead. "May I inquire what this is about?"

"It's a confidential matter," I said, "but I am most anxious to speak to Mr. Johansson regarding one of our policyholders. I think he could give me some valuable information."

"I understand," he said, nodding. "If you intend to be in Stockholm long, why not get in touch with me from time to time. It is possible that we will hear from Herr Johansson, and I will tell him that you wish to see him."

"You do that," I said.

I thanked him again, we shook hands, and I left the bank.

So far I had traveled several thousand miles to wind up on a dead-end street. I was certain that Jason Johansson was the C. Jackson, and Carl Johnson, that I wanted, but it wasn't going to do me much good unless I could find him. I needed to find some of his social contacts, even casual ones, if I expected to get a lead. It was possible that the business and the bank didn't know where he was, but it seemed apparent that they wouldn't tell me if they did know.

At the moment that left me with one possible source of information—the restaurant the banker had mentioned. I looked it up in the phone book and saw that it was not far away. It was almost lunchtime, so I decided to walk to it. I asked a policeman the direction and set off.

It was a large, handsome restaurant with a huge bar off to one side of the dining room. I went into the bar. There were five men sitting together in the center of the bar and a beautiful blonde all alone at one end of the bar. I took a stool about halfway between them. The bartender came over to ask me what I wanted. I told him a martini and he went off to mix it.

"American?" he asked when he came back with the drink.

I admitted I was, and tasted the martini. It was fine and I told him so. It obviously pleased him.

"Has Herr Johansson been in recently?" I asked him.

"Herr Jason Johansson? You know him?"

"I've never met him, but I came to Stockholm especially to see him. His office does not know where he is, but I heard that he often comes here."

"He has not been here in perhaps two weeks," the bartender said, "so he must be out of the country. He travels much of the time, but when he is in Stockholm he is here almost every day."

"Do you remember if he said where he was going the last time he was in?"

He shook his head. "Herr Johansson is a very friendly man, and I have had many long talks with him, but never about his business. He did not talk about that in here. This was the place where he came to relax, not to talk business. We try to respect such feelings in our customers."

"An excellent way to run an establishment," I agreed.

He must have received a signal from the blonde, for he excused himself and went over to her. They talked in low tones and I busied myself with my martini. I had almost finished it when the bartender came back. He had a worried look on his face.

"Fröken Kerstin Lindborg asks if you would like to join her and buy her a drink." He seemed embarrassed. "I should explain, sir, that she is not the sort of girl that she might appear to be from that. There are not what you would call professionals in here. She is a fine girl and has been coming to this restaurant for three or four years."

"I understand," I said. "I will be delighted to join Fröken Lindborg, and I will not misunderstand. Please make another martini for me and bring her whatever she likes."

I finished what was in my glass and walked down to the end of the bar. *"Goddag,* Fröken Lindborg," I said. "I am called Milo March. Would you do me the honor of having a drink with me?"

She laughed. "I speak better English than you do Swedish," she said. It was true. She had no real accent; only the lilt of her voice betrayed her original language. "And it is I who asked you to come drink with me. My friends call me Kerstin."

"And mine call me Milo," I said. Now that I was next to her I could see that she was even prettier than I had thought from a distance.

The bartender brought the drinks and then retired to the other end of the bar.

"You are wondering why I asked you to buy me a drink?" she said.

"Naturally," I said. "I am not, however, thinking what many men might think. I do think that you want something from me—but it's not me and it's not my money."

She laughed again. "And you want something from me—but you do not yet know what it is."

"Then I have a pleasant surprise ahead of me."

She raised her glass. *"Lycka till,"* she said.

"Good luck," I responded, and we clinked glasses, then drank.

"I heard you talking to the bartender," she said. "You are looking for the great Herr Jason Johansson?"

"I am."

"Are you a friend of his?"

"I have never met him."

"You are an American?"

"Yes."

"From what part of America?" she asked.

"I live in New York City."

"And what business are you in?"

"Insurance."

"And you have come all this way to see Herr Johansson, whom you don't even know?"

"Yes," I said.

"You must be very smart, Milo."

"Why do you say that?"

"Herr Johansson," she said slowly, "is a pig, a dirty pig. But he is also very smart. So if you followed him here, you must be even smarter. That is good."

"I'm afraid that I don't understand," I said.

"You understand," she said, laughing. "Now, take me into the dining room, buy me a few more drinks and some lunch, and I might just tell you some things you would like to know. Are you a gambler, Milo?"

"I'm a gambler," I said, "but never on women, for they always win. Sometimes you can expect a horse to fall down or lose his jockey or not find a hole along the rail, but a woman—never."

I beckoned the bartender over and paid him. Then I escorted the girl into the dining room. We took a corner table and I ordered two more drinks. We talked about Stockholm while we had the drinks and during lunch. Then we had coffee and brandy.

"You want to know where Jason is?" she asked suddenly.

"I'd like to," I admitted.

"You want to pay something?" she asked. There was a challenge in her voice.

"Not to you," I said. "I might to an informer, but that's different. That's not you. If you want to tell me anything, you will. If you don't, you won't. It's as simple as that. I will make no decisions with you. You must make them. You are both beautiful and intelligent, and if you want to tell me something you will do so. If you don't want to, we'll just enjoy our coffee and our brandy and after that we may go on somewhere else and we may not. In the latter case, we will say good-bye and it will have been a most pleasant day, and we will remember it as such."

There was a strange look on her face as she gazed at me. "You really mean that, don't you?"

"Of course. I cannot force you to do something you don't want to do. And I refuse to try to buy you. If you want to talk, fine. If you don't want to talk, fine. Then we'll just enjoy ourselves."

"You mean that too, don't you?" she asked.

"Of course I do. It is impossible to force people to do things they don't want to do—unless you want to start putting burning splinters under their fingernails. I'm not the type for that. It makes me sick at my stomach."

Suddenly she laughed. It wasn't a fun laugh, but it was a laugh. "All right," she said. "Let's enjoy the day and forget that there was ever such a person as Jason Johansson. We just met. I like you and you like me. We will have fun and that is all."

"It sounds like a wonderful idea," I said. "Where do we go next?"

"I know just the place," she said. "Shall we go?"

"By all means," I said. I signaled for the waiter and paid the check. We went outside and hailed a taxi. She gave him the address.

Eventually we ended up in a nightclub that was exactly like five thousand other nightclubs but that the girls were more undressed—except possibly in Paris. The table was small—as they always are—and we had to sit close together—as you always do—and before the floor show was over we were holding hands. The music was a Swedish version of American jazz, which also helped.

It was after midnight when we left.

"Where now?" I asked as we waited for a taxi.

"I don't know about you," she said with a giggle, "but I think I have stayed up too late and had too much to drink. I think you had better take me home."

"It is a pleasure," I said.

A taxi pulled up and she gave the driver the address. It was no more than a twenty-minute drive. I was going to tell the driver to wait when he pulled up in front of a very modern apartment building, but she beat me to it.

"Would you like to come up for a last drink?" she asked.

"I'm always ready for a last drink," I said gravely.

I paid the driver and we went into the building and took the elevator to the third floor.

Her apartment was small but it was attractive and well furnished. She immediately poured two drinks and we sat down in the kitchen to have them. She kicked off her shoes.

"*Lycka till,*" she said, lifting her glass.

"I've already had good luck," I said, lifting my own glass. "To you, Kerstin." We both took a healthy drink.

"Do you mind if I get comfortable?" she asked.

"Of course not," I said.

She stood up and went into the bedroom. I continued to work on my drink. After a bit I heard a soft sound behind me.

"Now I feel much better," she said as she passed me. I took a look—and then did a double take. She had removed all of her clothes—and had not replaced them. She sat down at the table and picked up her drink.

"Well, you certainly got comfortable," I said. "I am not, however, quite certain that it makes *me* comfortable."

She laughed, a soft sound in her throat. "Then you can go take your clothes off. There are plenty of hangers in my bedroom. And then we will be the same, eh?"

"Equal, perhaps," I said, "but not quite the same, thank goodness. Or maybe goodness has nothing to do with it." I thought about her suggestion and decided it was a good one. You may feel silly sitting around and having a drink with your clothes off, but not as silly as you do sitting there fully dressed across from a nude broad. I went into her bedroom and took my clothes off. I plucked a package of cigarettes and matches from my coat and went back to the kitchen—feeling pretty foolish about the whole thing.

She looked me over as I came into the room. "You are a very handsome man," she said as I sat down. "Perhaps you should never wear clothes."

"It might cause problems," I said.

I lit a cigarette and picked up my drink in an effort to be nonchalant. Then I thought to hell with it and took a good look at her. It was worth it. She had a wonderful body; everything in the right place and the right size.

"You like?" she asked.

"I like," I said. That was an understatement. She had large, firm breasts that stood straight out. Her stomach was flat until there was just a slight oval before it reached the loins. Her hair was reddish-blond and silky. Her hips were just wide enough, with generous curves in the rear, and her legs were long and tapering.

She stood up. "If you like," she said, "why do you not kiss me?" She came over and sat on my lap. What could I do except kiss her? As a matter of fact, after kissing her, I could think of only one thing better that I could have done. We left the drinks and the cigarettes and moved into the bedroom.

Later—much later—she propped herself up on one elbow and looked at me. "We were good?" she asked.

"We were very good," I said. "We were the very best."

She leaned over and nibbled briefly on my cheek. Then she sat up. "Would you like a drink or coffee?"

"Both," I said.

She pulled at me and we both got out of bed and went into the kitchen. She poured me a drink, put a cigarette in my mouth, and lit it. Then she started the coffee.

"I could make breakfast here," she said. "I am a good cook."

"I'm sure you are," I said. I was feeling very satisfied with the world. "But why should you slave over a hot stove? We'll go out to the best place you can think of."

"You are rich?"

"No, but my company is and they'll pay for it."

"Good," she said. She went back to watch the coffee. When it was done, she poured out two cups and brought them over. "I remember from lunch," she said. "You like yours without cream or sugar."

"Right," I said.

She put a small amount of sugar in her coffee and stirred it. Suddenly she lifted her head and looked at me. "Now I will tell you about the pig," she said.

"The pig?" I asked. To tell the truth, I had forgotten the reason we had started talking.

"Johansson," she said, spitting his name out.

"Oh," I said.

She laughed. "It is good that you acted that way. I was afraid that you only made love to me so that I would talk."

"You must be joking," I said. "As far as I am concerned, my only reason for being in Stockholm was to meet you."

"That is good," she said. She took one of my cigarettes and lit it. "You are looking for him because he went to America a few months ago, yes?"

"Yes," I admitted.

"I was there with him," she said.

I hadn't expected that, but I thought about it for a minute. "You," I said finally, "are Ann Brent."

It was her turn to look surprised. "Yes. It was his idea because I speak English well. But I didn't know the terrible things he was going to do."

"What do you mean?"

"We were in a city called—Philadelphia, is that right?"

"Yes."

"He made me go to bed with a man there—as if I were a whore. Then I heard later that the man killed himself. It was terrible. When I spoke to Jason about it, he merely laughed at me. And he had been telling me that he loved me. Can you imagine?"

"From what I know of him, I can imagine," I said.

"You want to find him?" she asked.

"Yes."

"Why?"

"Well," I said, taking a deep breath, "there are several reasons. First, in all honesty, it is my job, but I've become involved in it. One nice guy disappeared. I don't know whether he's dead or not. But I do know that there are four other men who are dead. If they hadn't died, they would have been ruined. I don't like your Herr Johansson."

"I also do not like him," she said. "Once I did, but no more. What will you do if you find him?"

"I don't know," I said honestly. "If I can, I will try to get him back to the United States for trial. If I can't, I don't know. I may kill him."

A slight shudder ran over her body. "He is a bad man," she said. "What do you want to know?"

"Whatever you know," I said.

"He has another company," she said, "and spends much of his time there. It is in Paris. The company is known as Jason Chimique Société, but I do not know what name he uses there. I'm sure it is not Johansson. He travels most of the time and he keeps most of his money in Switzerland."

"Johansson got something very valuable in Connecticut," I said, "and the man who invented it disappeared. He was either killed or kidnapped. Do you know anything about that?"

"No," she said. "I know that he was only kidnapped at first. I don't know what happened after that. But Jason was responsible for the death of the four men in your Philadelphia."

"Did you know Joe Pitcher?" I asked.

"He was what you call a creep," she said, "but he worked for Jason. I do not think he was a nice man."

"That is certainly one way of putting it," I admitted. "Does Johansson have a house or an apartment in Paris?"

"Yes, but I do not know where it is. He would never tell me. From the way he acted, I am also sure that he uses another name there."

"Why do you think so?"

"Once he had too much to drink. I said that if I got lonely I would send him a message at his Paris company. He laughed and told me not to bother because no one would know who to give it to. So he must use another name."

"But he is Swedish?"

"Yes. But he speaks five or six languages like a native, so I suppose he can pretend to be almost anything."

"I know one thing about him," I said. "He specializes in stealing inventions, both industrial and military. I gather that the industrial processes are put through his company here, and I would imagine that he sells the others to the highest bidder. How many people in the company are involved in it or know about it?"

"I do not know," she said. "I think that at the most it would be only the manager—perhaps not even him. Jason is not a man to share his secrets—or his money. It may be that even the manager believes that he buys the inventions he brings back."

One thing bothered me. "Why did he let you know so much about his business?"

"My father," she said, "worked for him. Jason claimed that my father stole money from the company. My father says that he did not, but he cannot prove it. I became Jason's mistress to keep my father from going to prison. And Jason used me in America, feeling sure that I would never betray him. That was bad enough. But in America he made me go to bed with another man. I will not go into court and destroy my father, but I think perhaps you will destroy Jason. … And you made love—glorious love—to me without asking any questions or making any demands."

"I will do my best," I said, "but not because we made love."

"That is why I talked to you."

"Where can I find him?"

"I don't know, Milo," she said. "I only know the name of the French company."

"Joe Pitcher," I said, more to myself than to her, "was certainly not his only employee, nor were you the only person he used by other means."

"You must be right," she said. "But I don't know who they are—and I'm sure they all have even less information than I have. He was careless with me a few times because he felt that I would do nothing against him. I wouldn't have—if he hadn't made me become a whore."

"I understand," I said gently. "Now, suppose we get dressed, go out, and have the finest breakfast Stockholm can boast."

"All right, Milo." She stood up and then kissed me on the cheek.

We both took showers and dressed. Then we went out on the town.

It was quite a day. I had never been in Stockholm before, but she certainly gave me a grand tour. Finally we went back to her apartment.

It was even better the second time. She wanted me to stay—and I wanted to—but there was still a lot of work ahead of me, so I used enough will power to say no. I told her that I would come back and see her to tell her what happened. Then I got dressed, kissed her on the mouth, and slipped out of the apartment while she was falling asleep.

It was midnight and the street was pretty much deserted. There wasn't a taxi in sight. I waited a few minutes, then decided I should try to find a taxi stand. I started briskly down the street.

I heard a car start up behind me, but I didn't think much about it at first. Then I heard the snarl of the motor, showing that the driver was accelerating as fast as he could. I'd had enough experience with that sound before not to be fooled into thinking that it was merely a driver in a hurry to get home.

I looked around. It was a small European car and there were two men in it. I suddenly realized that the passenger on my side of the car was leaning out of the window and the street light was glinting on something in his hand. The realization of this had barely materialized when there was a flash of red from his hand—and a bullet whistled past my head and splattered against the wall.

SEVEN

That was the only warning I needed. I hit the sidewalk, roll-ing toward the nearest building. Another bullet bounced off the sidewalk and screamed off into the night. I had no right to carry a gun in Sweden, so I did not have my regular gun with me. But I don't like to feel naked, so I did have a gun. It was an old American four-barreled derringer, which a gunsmith had adapted to use modern ammunition. It was tucked under my belt.

It was in my hand as I stopped rolling. The passenger in the car had just fired his second shot and was still leaning out of the window. I couldn't see what he looked like, but I could see his outline. I steadied the gun and squeezed the trigger. I saw him jerk as if he had been hit, and then the little car picked up speed, made a quick left turn, and disappeared.

Lights came on in several apartments on the street, and I decided it might be a good idea for me to get out of the neigh-borhood. I got up, ran to the first street, and turned right. I slowed down to a fast walk, made three more turns, and finally found a taxi. I gave the driver the name of my hotel and relaxed against the back seat. I was well away from the neigh-borhood before any alarm could be given. I went directly to my room and went to sleep.

When I awakened the next morning, I called room service

and ordered some breakfast and a newspaper. I took a quick shower while I was waiting for the food. The waiter came in shortly after I was out of the shower. I looked through the newspaper while I had breakfast. I found it on the third page. A man named Rolf Lindholm had been found on the street early in the morning. He'd been shot through the head and apparently thrown from a speeding car. There were no witnesses and no clues. The dead man did have a record. He had served time in both Sweden and France. The police had decided, according to the newspaper, that he must have antagonized some of his associates and had been killed by them.

I phoned and made a reservation on a plane to Paris. The first flight I could get was in the early afternoon. Then I phoned Kerstin Lindborg. She said she would have lunch with me.

I got dressed and packed my clothes. Then I stopped downstairs at the desk and told them what time I would be checking out. I took a taxi to the airlines office and had it wait while I picked up my ticket. My next stop was the Stockholm office of Intercontinental. I was shown into the office of Herr Andersson, the local manager. He examined my credentials, shook my hand warmly, and assured me he was at my complete disposal—all in good but singsong English.

"What is it that I can do for you, Herr March?" he asked.

"I'm not sure you can do anything," I said. "I am leaving very shortly for Paris. But I am interested in a Jason Johansson who owns Jason Aktiebolag here in Stockholm. Do you know him?"

He pursed his lips. "Not personally, you understand. I know of the man. He is well known here. A very successful man. But he spends much of his time traveling, and I have never actually met him."

"If he has so much success, I imagine he also gets considerable publicity?"

"Oh, yes. His name often appears in the financial or society pages."

"I would like," I said, "to get a photograph of Herr Johansson. Do you suppose it could be arranged?"

"Of course," he said with a wave of his hands. "At once."

He picked up the phone and put through a call to a Stockholm newspaper which I recognized as the one I'd read that morning.

Several calls later Herr Andersson was sweating and looking distressed. "I do not understand," he said unhappily. "No one has a photograph of Herr Johansson. They all say that he does not like to have his picture taken."

"I don't blame him," I said. "How about the police? Perhaps they have a photograph of him."

"The police? Herr Johansson?" He looked stunned. It was obvious that Herr Andersson was an admirer of successful men. But he picked up the phone and made the call. He identified himself twice and finally got someone who would listen to his questions. He didn't look too happy as he listened to the answers. Finally he hung up and looked at me.

"They do not have any photographs either, but I'm afraid that they do not look upon Herr Johansson with too much pleasure. They say that he is suspected of international operations which are not in the best interests of the Crown."

"Did they say what sort of operations?"

He shook his head sadly. "They would not tell me. I can't understand it. Herr Johansson is thought so well of in the best of circles."

"Sometimes it happens that way," I said.

I thanked him and left his office.

Downstairs I found a taxi and asked the driver to take me to Herr Johansson's home. When we arrived, I asked the driver to wait.

It was a beautiful house, just outside of the city, perched on the edge of a small lake. I went up to the front door and knocked. After a time the door opened and an old woman looked out.

"Is this the home of Herr Johansson?" I asked in Swedish.

"Ja," she said.

"I met Herr Johansson recently when he was in America," I explained, "and now that I find myself in Sweden, I thought I would like to see him again."

"Så synd!" she exclaimed. "He will be most disappointed. Herr Johansson is not here. He and his friend stayed only a few days after returning from America and then left for Europe. I do not know when he will be back. He will, I am sure, be disappointed."

"I'm sure," I said. "You say he and his friend?"

"Yes. The sick gentleman. Herr Johansson was hoping that he might be helped by the waters of Europe."

"Do you remember the name of the sick gentleman?" I asked.

She shook her head. "I am sorry but I do not. I do not have a good memory for those foreign names. But he was very sick.

He was in a wheelchair all the time he was here and almost never spoke."

"That is too bad," I agreed. "When do you expect Herr Johansson back?"

"I do not know. Sometimes he sends me a message that he is coming and sometimes he merely arrives. I am only the housekeeper."

"Do you know where he is?"

"No, sir. Somewhere in Europe, but I do not know where. He never tells me."

"What do you do with his mail?"

"He doesn't get any mail here." She gave me a toothless grin. "Except from young ladies. Those stay here until he comes. Would you like to leave a message?"

"I guess not," I said. "I am leaving Stockholm today and I'll probably catch up with him before he returns. Thank you."

I went back to the taxi and told the driver to take me to the restaurant. It was time for lunch.

I had one martini in the bar and then Kerstin showed up. The bartender seemed to be happy that we were meeting again. So was Kerstin. In fact, we were all happy.

We had a couple of drinks together and then went into the dining room. We ordered more drinks and our lunch.

"Milo," she said when the waiter had gone, "you have made me feel good."

"How?"

"I didn't expect you to phone me. But you did and we are also having lunch together. I did not think it would happen. Is there something else you want to ask me about?"

"No," I said. It wasn't exactly true, but I thought it was better to play it that way. "I promised you that I would talk to you today, and I wanted to see you because I am going to Paris this afternoon."

"I will never see you again," she said sadly.

"You will," I told her. "I promise you. I will come back this way when I've finished."

She looked at me steadily for several seconds without speaking. "I think you mean it," she said then.

"I do."

"Even if you change your mind—thank you," she said. "I was reading the newspaper this morning when you phoned. Did you read it?"

"Yes."

"There was something in it about a man named Rolf Lindholm who had been shot and thrown out of a car. The place where he was found was only a few blocks from my apartment."

"Oh?"

"Just after you left," she said, "I heard what I thought were several gunshots out on the street."

"That must have been frightening," I said.

She smiled. "I thought you might be interested in knowing that I once met a Rolf Lindholm. He was with Jason Johansson. ... Of course, if you are not interested ..."

"I didn't say that I wasn't interested," I said.

"He tried to kill you, didn't he?" she asked. "And you killed him instead?"

I wasn't too sure of her, but I finally decided to be truthful.

"Yes," I said. "But I'd rather it wasn't talked about."

"Of course," she said. "I wouldn't say anything, Milo, except to you. I just wanted to tell you, if it is important, that Rolf Lindholm worked with Jason Johansson."

"They worked together?"

"Yes. Jason said that Lindholm worked for him. He didn't say what kind of work, but he did not appear to me to be a good man. He proved it last night if he tried to kill you. But how did he know about you? I said nothing to anyone."

"I believe you, honey," I said. "Your friend Jason left someone in America to cover his trail. He probably was warned that I was looking for him, so he left someone here to watch in case I showed up. In this case there were two men. Someone driving the car in which Lindholm was riding. There will probably be someone else in Paris."

She leaned forward and put her hand on mine. "Milo, please be careful. Jason is a dangerous man."

"I'm always careful," I told her. "Are you sure that he never gave you any idea of where he lived when he was in Paris?"

She shook her head. "The nearest he came was telling me I could get in touch with him through Jason Chimique Société."

"Under his own name?"

Well—he told me to send any messages to him at the company, but in care of another man."

"Remember the name of the other man?"

"I think his last name was Piquet—or something like that—but I'm not sure. It was more than a year ago. Then he told me never to send any messages there."

"And you did not send any?"

"Not after he told me I shouldn't."

"You were in love with him?" I asked gently.

"Not really," she said. "I was fascinated because of his strength and power. And after that I was frightened. I still am."

"But not too frightened to tell me about him?"

"Because I must be released from him," she said simply. "When I heard you asking about him here in the bar, I had a sudden feeling that you might be the one to do that. It was for that reason I had enough courage to speak to you."

"I'll try, honey," I said.

We finished our lunch and she went with me to the hotel. I got my luggage and checked out. She accompanied me to the airport and I gave her taxi money for the return trip. We had a final drink together and she walked to the gate with me. I kissed her gently on the mouth.

"*Adjö,*" I said.

"*Adjö,*" she repeated, "*Lycka till.*"

"*Tack,*" I said. "I will see you on my way home."

I stepped through the gate and walked to the plane without looking back. When we landed in Paris, I went through customs. I switched my small gun to a leg holster so it didn't show and no one was the wiser. I took a taxi to the Palais d'Orsay and registered. I had a bottle of good brandy sent up to my room and had a drink. Then I took a shower, shaved, and changed clothes. It was too late in the day to visit any offices. I stopped at the hotel bar and had a leisurely martini. Then I took a taxi to Le Cabaret. I had another cocktail, then the *blan-*

quette de veau à l'ancienne with a good bottle of wine, and after that a cheese with coffee and brandy. While I enjoyed it, I contemplated the advantages of an expense account.

After dinner I went to Le Caveau des Oubliettes and drank some more wine while I listened to old French songs. I was renewing my romance with Paris—and Martin Raymond should consider it money well spent, although he probably wouldn't if he had known about it. He was narrow-minded that way.

I took a taxi back to the hotel and went up to my room. I wasn't exactly ready for sleep, so I phoned downstairs and asked them to send up a newspaper. I took off my coat, poured a drink of brandy, and made myself comfortable.

A few minutes later there was a knock on the door. I went over and opened it.

He didn't look like a bellhop—even in Paris. He was too big. But I had very little time to evaluate him. When I opened the door he was standing there, holding the newspaper in one hand. In the other hand he was holding a knife. The point of the four-inch blade was quickly pressed against me, just above my belt. The impression of it was just enough to hurt a little and make my belly retreat to somewhere in the neighborhood of my spine. It was most uncomfortable.

EIGHT

Johansson was on the ball, I had to admit that. I'd barely landed in Paris when he had one of his boys there with a knife shoved against my belly. It was a nice philosophical point, but this was no time for philosophy.

"Je vous demande pardon," I said politely. At the same time I chopped my left hand across his wrist, twisted to one side, and swung a hard right at his jaw.

The knife slit through my shirt and I felt a slight burning across my side. Then my fist landed and he staggered back into the corridor.

Suddenly a new factor intruded. A roly-poly man erupted from the room next to mine and hit my attacker, knocking him to the floor.

"Lâche!" he shouted. *"Allez!"*

The man struggled to his feet, looking at both of us, then bolted for the stairway. His feet clattered on the steps.

"Allez!" my newfound assistant shouted after him.

"Merci," I said when he finally looked at me.

He beamed. *"Il n'y a pas de quoi,"* he answered. "It is fortunate that I happened to hear a noise and came out."

"Most fortunate," I agreed gravely. "But it is too bad we did not catch him for the police."

"C'est dommage!" he exclaimed. "I did not think, M'sieu,

except that he should be routed. A thousand pardons." He stared at me and his eyes widened. "But you are bleeding, M'sieu. We must call a doctor."

I glanced down and saw that my shirt was bloody. I unbuttoned it and looked at my flesh. There was a three-inch cut across my side, but it was no more than skin deep. It had almost stopped bleeding.

"It is nothing," I said. "A little cold water will fix it. I am grateful to you, M'sieu." I wasn't, but there was no point in telling a well-meaning man that he was a jerk.

He made a formal bow. "I am happy to have been of service. I am Jean Nicot. I am occupying the room next to you."

"I am Milo March," I said.

He frowned. "March? Then you are not French, yet you speak our language so well. You are, perhaps, English?"

"American."

"Ah, American!" he exclaimed, his face lighting up. "I have always been very fond of Americans."

"It is a feeling which I do not think is always shared by your leader," I said dryly. "In the meantime, may I make a suggestion?"

"By all means, M'sieu." He struck his forehead with his open hand. "But, of course. How stupid of me. I am chattering away while you stand there bleeding! May I help you, M'sieu?"

"I wasn't thinking of myself. I had asked them to send up a newspaper. The man who knifed me was carrying a newspaper, so it is possible that he had previously attacked the boy in order to get the paper. Do you know the direction of the service elevator?"

"I believe it is this way," he said uncertainly, pointing over his shoulder.

We walked down the corridor until we finally found it. The door was propped partly open. Just as we reached it, we heard a groaning from inside. I pushed the door open and there was a young man sitting on the floor and rubbing his head.

"Que diable!" exclaimed my companion.

Between us, we managed to get the boy to his feet, and he immediately began to blurt out his story. He had been hit over the head. He had not, however, seen the one who struck him. I finally stopped him by shoving some francs into his hand and suggesting he'd better get back downstairs and report what had happened to him.

On the way back down the corridor I realized that I had better do some reporting myself. The hotel manager would certainly call the police, and they might think it curious if I kept quiet about it. I swore under my breath.

"Comment?" Nicot asked.

"It is nothing," I said. "There was merely a bit of smarting along my side."

"Something must be done," he said. "Would you like to come into my room and I will call a doctor?"

"A doctor won't be necessary. I have some first-aid equipment in my room and that is all that should be necessary." I looked at him. He seemed like a nice little man—and he was my only witness. "Why don't you come into my room, M'sieu Nicot? I have some very good brandy, and the police will want to talk to both of us when they arrive."

"The police?"

"Of course. The manager will naturally call them when he hears the story of the boy, and as a responsible visitor to your country I should also report the incident."

"To be sure," he said. "I had not thought of it in that light. I will accept your kind invitation."

He checked that he had his key, then closed the door to his room. We went into mine. I poured two drinks and handed one to him. I lifted my glass.

"Your health, M'sieu. It showed great courage to come to my assistance as you did."

"It was nothing" he said modestly. "To your health, M'sieu March."

We drank.

"Now, if you'll excuse me for a minute," I said. I stripped off my bloody shirt and looked at the wound. It wasn't bad and had already stopped bleeding. I took a first-aid kit from my luggage and went into the bathroom. I washed off the blood, sterilized the wound, covered it up with gauze, and taped it. I went back to the room, put on a fresh shirt, and then picked up the telephone. When the operator answered, I asked for the manager.

"*Oui?*" he answered a moment later.

"M'sieu Milo March in Room 300," I said. "Earlier I asked to have a newspaper sent up. When there was a knock on the door, I opened it. There was a man there with my news-paper, but he also had a knife with which he attacked me. Fortunately, the gentleman in the room next to me came to my aid and the assassin fled. We then discovered that the young man who was bringing my newspaper had also been attacked in the service elevator. He may have reported to you by this time. I hope you understand, M'sieu, that I am not in any way blaming the hotel for this, but I think I should report it to you and to the police."

"*Merde,* M'sieu," he said. "Are you seriously injured?"

"Only a mere scratch. It is nothing."

"We are happy for you. I have already reported to the police, and there should be someone here at any moment. You will be in your room, M'sieu?"

"Yes. M'sieu Nicot is also here with me. We will be available." I hung up and replenished our drinks. "The manager has already notified the police, and I suppose they will soon be here. I am sorry you are to be further inconvenienced."

"It is nothing," he said with a shrug. "I am only sorry that a guest of our country must meet such treatment." He hesitated. "I do not mean to intrude, M'sieu, but why should someone attack you like that? Have you made an enemy since you have been here—perhaps because of a woman?"

"I just arrived—a few hours ago. You are the first person I have met since arriving, unless one counts waiters and taxi drivers. Perhaps he merely thought I was a rich American."

"It is possible," he said. "May one inquire, M'sieu, if you are here on business or pleasure?"

"Of course you may. It is a business trip, but I hope I will also have some pleasure, M'sieu Nicot."

"Please forgive me, but I know that in your country you have the pleasant custom of informality. You would honor me if you called me Jean."

"All right. Call me Milo."

"I am honored." He hesitated again. "I am from southern France, but I find it necessary to come to Paris often on business, so I know the city well. If I may be of any assistance in your search for pleasure, or in your business, please feel free to call on me."

"I'll remember that," I said. "What business are you in, Jean?"

"Wines. In fact, I am part-owner of the company which makes this brandy you are serving me. But my chief business is in wines."

"An excellent business," I said, filling the glasses again. "I drink to it." I did.

"You are in international trade, Milo?" he asked.

"In a way." I decided I might as well be more or less truthful, since I would have to be honest with the police. "I'm in insurance with a company that has an office in Paris." Intercontinental did have a small office in Paris, although I had never seen it.

"An interesting business," he said politely.

We had another drink apiece and talked about France and America until there was a knock on the door. I went to answer it. The man who stood there was small and thin, wearing a wrinkled suit and a tired expression. "M'sieu March?" he asked.

I admitted I was.

He looked a little happier. "Ah, you speak French. That is good. I am Maurice Carot from the Brigade Criminelle. May I come in?"

I stepped aside and let him enter the room. I introduced

him to Jean Nicot and then waved him to the only other chair in the room. I offered him a brandy. He accepted so quickly that I suspected there was a simple reason for his tired expression. I poured a drink for him and refilled Nicot's glass as well as my own. I sat on the bed and lit a cigarette.

"I am sorry to have bothered you so late, Inspecteur."

"I am only a detective," he said wearily. "You were attacked this evening, M'sieu?" He pulled a notebook and pencil from his pocket.

"Yes," I said. "I had called downstairs and asked them to send up a newspaper. When the knock came, I opened the door and saw a man with a newspaper in his hand. But there was a knife in his other hand, and the point of it was immediately pressed against my stomach. I struck his arm and then hit him in the face. At this point, M'sieu Nicot came to my assistance and knocked the man down. He immediately got to his feet and ran away before we could stop him."

"Could you describe him, M'sieu March?"

"Not as well as I would like to," I admitted. "It happened so quickly. He was a tall man; I would say only slightly under six feet. He weighed somewhere between one hundred and seventy-five and one hundred and ninety pounds. Very black hair, moderately long. Clean-shaven. I didn't notice any special markings on his face. I would guess that he was, perhaps, in his middle thirties."

"You were wounded, M'sieu?"

"Yes."

"To what extent?"

I opened my shirt and showed him the bandage. "It is only

skin deep. Nothing serious." I went into the bathroom and returned with my bloody shirt. "This was the shirt I was wearing at the time."

He made a soft clucking sound in his throat. "It is regrettable that you are welcomed to France in such a fashion. You are an American, no?"

"Yes."

"You are here, perhaps, on a business trip?"

"That is correct."

"May one ask what business engages your interest?"

"I am in insurance. Intercontinental Insurance. It is an American company, although there is a branch office in Paris as well as in other European cities."

"Is it possible to inquire the exact reason for your visit to Paris?"

"If it becomes necessary," I said carefully, "I will make a complete statement, but I do not believe it is needed. Until it is, I prefer not to go into details. You know how much competition there is in international business."

"You do not see any connection between this attack and your reason for being in Paris?"

"How can I?" I asked. "Insurance is a very peaceful business. Perhaps the man merely thought I was a rich American and he could rob me."

"Of course," he said. He didn't look as if he believed it. He turned his gaze on Jean Nicot. "Your statement about this unfortunate incident, M'sieu Nicot?"

Nicot verified most of what I had said. He told of hearing a noise in the corridor and opening his door in time to see the man reeling back from my blow. He had rushed out and struck the assailant, who had thereafter escaped. The two of us had found the bellboy in the service elevator. I had reported the crime. We had then waited for the arrival of the formidable detective. He also identified himself and produced his various papers.

The detective sighed and put away his notebook. "Yes, yes," he said. "Sometimes it is like this. We shall see. You will be in Paris for a few days, M'sieu March?"

"I expect to be."

"And you, M'sieu Nicot?"

"Yes," he said. "A week, perhaps longer."

He finished his brandy and stood up. He looked at me and for the first time something like a smile appeared on his face. "You know," he said, "I could have had an appointment in the postal department, but I turned it down because I thought it would be too hard on my feet. I never knew that detectives walked so much. Good night, gentlemen."

I went to the door with him and then returned to my guest. We had one more drink, which finished the bottle. Nicot wanted us both to go out and visit a nightclub that he recommended, but I begged off. I'd had enough to drink and I was tired. We parted in everlasting friendship and I went to sleep.

In spite of the brandy, I felt pretty good when I awakened the following morning. I had breakfast in my room, including some lovely scrambled eggs. They sent up a paper with my breakfast. It was only a small story, but there was my name on one of the inner pages. I could have done without that.

Later I took a taxi to the offices of Jason Chimique Société.

They were nice offices. There was a lovely-looking French girl who was the receptionist, and there was a small, nondescript man sitting on a chair in obvious hopes of seeing someone. I went up to the receptionist and tried out my best smile.

"There is nothing like Paris in the spring," I said brightly.

"Pardon?" she said. It was the sort of witty remark I could have expected on Madison Avenue.

"Maybe it isn't spring," I said. "Let's start all over again. My name is Milo March. I am an American. I have come all this way to see Jason Johansson. Would it be possible?"

She looked puzzled. "M'sieu Johansson? Are you sure that is whom you wish to see?"

"Quite sure," I said firmly.

She shrugged and picked up her phone. She talked at some length concerning me and my problem. Finally she replaced the phone and gave me a mechanical smile.

"If you will be seated, M'sieu, someone will be out to see you."

I nodded—there was nothing else to do—and took a seat across from the other man who was waiting. Looking at him did not cheer me up. He had the appearance of having been there for weeks waiting for someone to show up.

To my surprise, however, it was only a few minutes before a tall, slim, immaculate man came into the reception room. A glance from the eyes of the receptionist sent him in my direction.

"M'sieu March?" he asked, making a slight bow in front of me.

"I think so," I said, standing up. "You are … ?"

"I am Jacques Maquet, manager of Jason Chimique Société, at your service, M'sieu."

"I wanted to see a Jason Johansson."

"I do not understand," he said. "We have no one by that name in this company."

"You're sure?"

"I am certain, M'sieu. I have been the manager here for more than ten years, and there has never been anyone here by that name."

"Aren't you connected with Jason Aktiebolag of Sweden?"

He pursed his lips. "Connected, no. Sometimes we do business with them, as we do with other companies throughout the world, but that is all."

"Who is the owner of this company?" I asked.

"Georges Piquet."

"And what is the principal business of your company?"

"I do not understand the reason for your questions," he said. "We are a well-known and well-respected firm. Our business has always been the same. We deal primarily in various plastic products and in drugs. Our products are known all over Europe."

I had a sudden idea. "Tell me, M'sieu Maquet, have you recently begun to market a plastic that is stronger than steel and, perhaps, a new drug for the treatment of arthritis?"

He looked surprised. "Of course. We are already doing quite well with those two items, although I was not aware that their fame had spread so far as America."

"And did you also happen to purchase or lease the patents on those two products?"

"We lease almost all of our products. That is, we lease rights to the European market. It is seldom that we are able to get world rights. Patent-holders like to deal with various companies."

"I don't suppose that you just happened to lease those particular patents from Jason Aktiebolag in Stockholm?"

"As a matter of fact, I believe we did," he said with dignity, "but I assure you that it is a completely legitimate deal. We have done business with them for years, and everything has always been satisfactory."

"I wasn't questioning that," I said. "Who did you say was the owner of this company?"

"Georges Piquet."

"Could I see him?"

"I'm afraid it is impossible at the moment, M'sieu. He is out of the city."

"Where?"

He shrugged. "I do not know exactly. M'sieu Piquet spends most of his time traveling around the Continent, making sales contacts, obtaining new patents, representing the company wherever we do business."

"Doesn't everyone?" I asked. "When will he return?"

"I do not know, M'sieu. He gets in touch with the office when he feels like it, since he knows that this end of the business is run most efficiently. The other function is his province and is, I might say, the most important."

"I'm sure of it," I said. "It reminds me of other business-men I've heard about. May I ask a rather personal question? Could it be possible that M'sieu Piquet is about five feet nine and weighs in the neighborhood of one hundred and seventy-five pounds?"

He looked surprised again. "You have met him?"

"No, but I would like to," I said. "Well, I'll check with you."

"But, if it's business, M'sieu, I am empowered to discuss anything and to draw any contracts."

"I'm sure that's very nice," I said, "but I've already seen you. Now I want to see the man who is the head of the company. I will be back."

He was still looking puzzled as I left. It wasn't until I was down on the street that I realized that the little man who had been in the reception room had followed me out of the building. When I stopped, he came up to me.

"Je vous demande pardon," he said. "May I speak to you for a moment, M'sieu?"

"But certainly," I told him. "About what?"

He looked around the street. "This is not a good place to talk. There is a little café a block from here. Perhaps you would permit me to buy you a glass of wine and we could talk a few minutes there."

"All right," I said.

"It is called Marie's. It is on this street one block from here. I will go ahead and take a table, outside. We can talk there."

"Go ahead," I said.

He walked past me and continued on down the street. I gazed in a shop window for a few minutes, then walked in the same direction. I soon saw the place. It was a sidewalk café and the little man was seated at a table. There were only two other people there, and they were some distance from him. There were already two glasses of wine on his table. I took the chair across from him.

"I am Andre Chaland," he said.

"And I am Milo March," I answered.

He nodded. "I heard your name in the office. M'sieu, you are looking for a man who sometimes calls himself Jason Johansson?"

"You mean he has other names?" I asked, as if I didn't know.

"I think many names. I cannot prove it, but I think he is also the Georges Piquet mentioned to you by the manager."

"Why are you interested in this?" I asked bluntly.

"I am also trying to find him, M'sieu."

"Why?"

He stared at me for a minute. "Let us say that it was a business deal between us and that he did not quite live up to his part of the agreement."

"And when you find him?"

"I will kill him, M'sieu," he said softly.

"Well, that's a straight answer," I said. "In all honesty, I must admit that I don't much care what happens to him after I've finished my business with him. But I'm curious about one thing. Why do you come to me?"

He smiled but there was no humor in it. "Perhaps I can help you and perhaps you can help me. Since there are no witnesses, M'sieu, I will tell you that I care about nothing but the death of Johansson and I don't care how it is brought about. If you wish to kill him, I will think it an excellent idea. If you don't wish to go that far, then I ask only that you turn him over to me."

"What advantage is there for me in cooperating with you?"

"It is simple, M'sieu. We will exchange information. Whichever one of us finds him first, you will have a chance with him. But you in turn promise that when you are through with him, it will be my turn. That is all."

"That sounds fair," I said carefully. "What can you tell me now?"

"Not much," he admitted. "I know that he calls himself Johansson and Piquet, and I suspect that he uses many other names. I know that he steals many patents and inventions throughout the world. Those that are business matters are handled through the offices where I just saw you or through a company he owns in Sweden. Those which are of a more delicate nature he sells to the highest bidder. These, you understand, are countries. They might include countries such as Russia, but sometimes they might be countries which are considered friends of your country and mine. They, too, like to gain an advantage. You understand?"

"All too well," I admitted. "Is there anything else that you know about him?"

"Il a de l'or plein ses poches," he said simply. "He has his pockets full of gold. And I will know him if I see him."

"That is one advantage. I would still like to know why you want him so badly."

"I cannot tell you the exact reason, M'sieu. It is enough to say that we entered into a business arrangement. I performed my part of the arrangement. He did not do his."

"All right," I said. "I will make the agreement with you. At this point I do not know any more than you do. In fact, I know less, since I have never seen him. I am staying at the Palais d'Orsay and you can reach me there. How do I get in touch with you?"

"There is a little club called Ma Petite in the Montmartre section. You can always find me there or leave a message which I will get."

"All right." I finished my wine and stood up. "We will see each other."

"*Oui.*"

I left the café and walked a block down the street before I stopped to decide what I would do next. It didn't take me long to reach a decision. At that point, even after traveling several thousand miles, I had very little on the case. I had a shadowy villain, with only the vaguest description and no photograph. He was obviously a man with many names in many countries.

There was no doubt in my mind that he was an international thief and murderer—but I had to have more than my own conviction. Personally, I had enough proof that he was feeling pushed—from what had happened in New York, in Stockholm, and then the night before in Paris—but that alone would not bring the case to a solution. I decided that I would go to the Sûreté.*

There was a taxi stand across the street. I started over to the other side. I was halfway across the street when I heard a motor cough into life and then the sudden roar as it accelerated. Even then I didn't get it until the last minute, despite

---

* La Sûreté Nationale, the former name of La Police Nationale, was the criminal investigative bureau of Paris.

the incident in Sweden. There was a big black Citroën heading straight for me.

I threw myself to the pavement and rolled. My gun was in the leg holster and there was no opportunity to reach for it. I concentrated on two things: getting out of the path of the car and getting a look at the driver. I barely succeeded in both efforts.

The driver of the car was Joe Pitcher—the man I had last seen unconscious in a Greenwich Village courtyard in New York City after I had knocked him out.

NINE

The Citroën roared on down the street, and I picked myself up and brushed off my suit. Such is the fame of Paris drivers that no one paid any attention to me. I walked down to the first taxi in the line and climbed in.

The driver had obviously watched the whole incident. *"Il n'y a que les morts qui ne reviennent pas,"* he quoted with a shrug. "It is only the dead who do not return. Where do you next wish to try your luck, M'sieu?"

I told him, and this produced a different shrug, but it also made him keep quiet during the ride. He let me out in front of the building that housed the famous French police department and I went inside. It took some time, and considerable conversation, before I finally arrived at the floor of the Brigade Criminelle. There I was passed from the *officier de paix* to the *inspecteur principal* to the *brigadier* (something like a sergeant), and then I was finally sent to a small, airless office. There I found Detective Maurice Carot. He looked just as tired as he had the night before. He managed a small amount of animation at the sight of me.

"Ah," he said. "M'sieu March. I was about to see if you were at the hotel."

"I am not at the hotel," I said. "I am here."

"So you are," he observed.

He thrust his hand into a pile of papers on his desk and came up with a photograph and pushed it toward me. "Do you recognize this person?"

It was a very good picture of the man who had shown up at my room the night before with a newspaper and a knife.

"Yes," I said. "That's the man who attacked me last night. You have found him?"

"Yes, M'sieu. We found him this morning on the edge of the river—with his throat cut."

"That's nice. Do you think there is a connection?"

"We don't know. The man was a known criminal, so he may have been killed for any one of several reasons. But it is possible that there is a connection since it happened so soon after he attacked you." He took out a cigarette and made a ritual of lighting it. He stared at me through the cloud of smoke. "It is possible to suspect, M'sieu, that you were not completely honest with me last night concerning the attack."

"Everything is possible," I said lightly. "I was honest with you—as far as I went. I did not go farther for several reasons, one of them being that there was a third person present. I do represent an insurance company and I am here on business for them. It is possible that the attack on me last night was related to that, but the attacker was no one that I know, and I have absolutely no proof of any kind that there is a connection between the two things."

"But you think there is?"

I nodded. "I do. I am an insurance investigator. The case on which I'm working involves theft and the death of several persons. After I started working on the case, I was attacked in New York City, again in Stockholm, and finally here. My instinct tells me that they are all related, but I have no proof."

He puffed out another cloud of smoke and peered through it. "Do you have any authority in France, M'sieu?"

"None," I said cheerfully.

"But you have a reason for coming to see me today?"

"Yes."

"Is it possible," he asked sarcastically, "to ask what this reason is?"

"To exchange information."

"So?"

"Do you know anything about a man who calls himself Georges Piquet and who owns Jason Chimique Société here in Paris? I believe that he is also known as Jason Johansson and owns a company in Sweden known as Jason Aktiebolag."

"So far," he observed, "you are not exchanging information, M'sieu; you are merely trying to obtain information. There is a difference between what you suggest and what you do."

I smiled at him. "You misunderstand me. If I am careful, it is because you have not yet said that you would exchange information or cooperate in any way. I did not come here to make you a present of anything. My heart is not that big."

He waved the smoke away from his face, then suddenly leaned back and laughed. "I like you, M'sieu. You are not like the Americans I have met. I will exchange information with you. We do have a certain interest in Georges Piquet, and we have had suspicions that he uses other names, but we have no proof of any kind against him. It is only that we are interested in him and his activities."

"I tried to see him at his company today but was told he was out of the city."

He shrugged. "He is out of the city most of the time, M'sieu. It is not certain what he does, although it is claimed he is representing his company."

"I believe," I said, "that he is an international thief of patents and inventions—industrial and sometimes, perhaps, military."

"Our suspicions are along the same lines," he said, "but as I told you, we have no proof. We would be grateful for any information you could give us."

"I don't have any yet—beyond what I've told you. Is there a photograph of him?"

He grimaced. "He has never been arrested in France, so there is no official photograph. In addition, he seems to have an aversion to the camera, and we do not know of any photographs of him. We tried to find one when we were preparing a file on him."

"Do you know a man named Andre Chaland?" I asked.

"That one I know," he said. "He has been arrested many times. He has not been in prison as many times as he should have been. He deals in anything that will make a profit—robbery, theft, blackmail, pimping, assault, and, I think, murder—but some of these charges we have not been able to prove."

"Do you have any evidence that Chaland ever had any connection with Piquet?"

He looked surprised. "No. Why?"

"Chaland is also looking for Piquet. I talked to him. He

would not tell me the reason he wanted him, but he did mention that there had been a business arrangement in which Piquet did not live up to his part of the bargain. In view of what you have told me about Chaland, this would sound as if he had been double-crossed by Piquet."

"That sounds as if it were true," the detective said. "I will see if we can learn anything about it. Do you expect to see Chaland again?"

"Yes. He offered some sort of cooperation, and I don't see that I have anything to lose. I will keep you informed of anything that I learn."

"And you want in return?"

"Information and cooperation, as I've already said. If I am right in thinking that Piquet is also Johansson, then my government will want to extradite him for murder and grand larceny—and possibly on charges of committing espionage. That, of course, will have to be handled through channels."

"Very proper," he said, nodding. "Even though you are not a regular police official of your country, I see no reason why we cannot cooperate—at least up to the point of the actual apprehension."

I laughed. "Cops sound the same no matter where they come from. What you're really saying is that I can do as much of your dirty work as possible and then maybe you'll throw me a crumb. But if that's the only way you'll play ..."

His face had tightened. "I do not like the way that you speak, M'sieu March. I know about you Americans, especially those from Chicago. Do you come from there?"

"No."

"Have you come here," he asked sternly, "with the idea that you can do as you please, like those private detectives in the novels we import from America?"

"Of course not."

"Do you have a gun with you, M'sieu?"

I threw open my coat. "Do you see one?"

"No, but that is not what I asked. Do you have a gun with you? If so, it is against the law."

"The question is so silly that I refuse to answer it. After all, I came through the French customs, and surely they are efficient enough to discover a gun if I were smuggling one into the country."

That stopped him for a few seconds but no longer. "It is always possible that there is an error," he said finally. He tried to look official again. "If you possess a weapon, M'sieu, I demand that you give it to me at once."

"Why?"

That also stopped him briefly. "It—it's against the law," he said lamely.

"What is?"

"For a foreigner to carry a gun in our country."

"Do you see me carrying a gun?"

"No."

"Did I say I was carrying a gun?"

"No."

"Then why do you try to push me around?" I asked. "We were speaking of more important matters. Do you know of a place in Paris called Ma Petite?"

"I know it," he said grimly. "It is a place where you can buy almost anything—including murder. Andre Chaland spends much of his time there."

"That is where he told me to get in touch with him."

"It is a place where you can find many like Chaland, including a man from your country."

"Who is he?"

"He is known as Doc Black, alias Blackie. His specialty is women, but he goes in for other things as well."

"Do you know of an American here by the name of Joseph Pitcher?"

He gnawed on his upper lip. "I do not recall the name. Has he been here long?"

"Not now, although he may have been here before. I believe that he has just arrived. I saw him in New York a few days ago, and then I saw him here as I was on my way to see you. I'm pretty certain that he is connected with Piquet. At least, if Piquet is Johansson."

"I will look into his presence."

"You say," I continued, "that you have been watching Piquet. He only recently returned to Paris after an absence of some time, did he not?"

"Yes."

"Do you know if he was alone when he arrived, or was there someone with him?"

"I will find out," he said.

He picked up his phone and talked for a few minutes to someone. He replaced the phone and looked at me.

"There was someone with him. A man named Nilsson who carried a Swedish passport and was an invalid. He was in a wheelchair. Piquet explained that Nilsson was a friend of his and was being brought here for medical treatment."

"Piquet explained? Why didn't the man explain for himself?"

"As I understand it, the man was under heavy sedation. Piquet said that the man was in great pain and that his Swedish doctor had given him the sedation so that he could make the trip. His papers were in order and there was nothing of a suspicious nature in his luggage. Why are you interested in this, M'sieu?"

"I think it is related," I said. I had a feeling of excitement about this one piece of news. "Did this Nilsson leave with Piquet when he went abroad again?"

"Apparently not. Piquet left for West Germany and was alone."

"May I make a suggestion?"

"By all means, M'sieu."

"If Nilsson is still in Paris—and since he is here on a foreign passport, there must be a record of where he is, whether it is a hospital, a hotel, or an apartment house—perhaps he can be located. We might learn more."

"It will be done. Of course, there will be no record if he is staying with friends. Or let us say that there might not be an accurate record. It is also possible that he is staying in Piquet's apartment, but we will check that."

"Thank you," I said. "I have already taken up too much of your valuable time. We will be in touch with each other."

"I trust that this is so," he said firmly. "I will expect to hear from you."

"You will."

I left and wandered through various corridors until I finally reached the street. I found a taxi and went back to my hotel. I dropped in at the bar and had a couple of drinks. As I passed the desk, I noticed that there was a message or a letter for me. I stopped and asked for it.

Once I was in my room, I looked at the note. It was from Jean Nicot, asking if I would join him for dinner and saying that he would phone me later to see if I could make it. Well, it left me plenty of time. I undressed and took a cooling shower. Then I lit a cigarette and stretched out on the bed.

The way I saw it, there was a good chance that Angus Watson, the missing inventor, was still alive. Johansson might just have been able to take him from the United States to Sweden and then to France. And Watson and his invention would be what he was trying to sell to the highest bidder—if he hadn't already sold them. The only problem was to find Watson, if possible, before he was sold.

I had an idea. I phoned downstairs and ordered a bottle of brandy and some ice. I also ordered some lunch, but told them to wait an hour before they sent it up. I stretched out on the bed again until there was a knock on the door. This time I was careful when I opened the door, but it was a waiter. He brought in the brandy and ice, and I paid him.

When he left, I fixed a drink and then I went to my coat pocket and found a small book I carried. It was full of phone numbers, most of them coded. I found the one I wanted and asked the operator to get it for me. It was an unlisted number, but the bill was paid by the CIA—no matter who signed the check.

"I would like to speak to M'sieu Henri Flambeau," I said when a girl answered.

There was a second of silence. "Who is calling?" she asked then.

"Tell him it's Milo from W," I said.

"Just a minute," she said. "I'll see if we have anyone by that name here."

I waited, hoping that this meant he was in Paris. Henri Flambeau was a Frenchman who worked for the CIA. We had done many jobs together and were good friends.

"Milo!" a voice said on the phone. It was Henri. *"Il y avait un jeune homme de Provence ..."*

"Dont les couilles étaient vraiment immenses," I finished. It was part of a naughty old limerick we both enjoyed.

He laughed loudly. *"Mon ami,* what are you doing in Paris? They put you back to work?"

"No," I said. "Are you busy at the moment, Henri?"

"Not too busy for you, my friend. Why?"

"I'm at the Palais d'Orsay. Come over as soon as you can."

"I'll be there in a few minutes."

He was as good as his word. In about fifteen minutes there was a knock on the door, and there he was. We embraced each other and I pulled him into the room and closed the door. I poured a brandy for him and we gazed fondly at each other.

"My dear friend," he said, "I am sure you would try to get in touch with me if you were over here as a tourist, but I have a feeling that is not the case. Yet you say that you have not been put back to work, nor have I received any information that such is the case. So, first, tell me what is going on and then we will have a reunion."

"It's a little odd," I said. "I'm working on a civilian case, but it is one in which there is a certain amount of interest in other quarters. In fact, I was asked by an important mutual friend to see what I could do, but he not only offers no cooperation, his trained seals get in my way. He has told them to give me no help at all; you may have received similar orders."

"I have received none," he said simply. "If I had, it would make no difference. You and I have been through too much together. What can I do for you, Milo?"

"I don't know. Perhaps we can do something for each other. The only part of my job that concerns you involves a brilliant young electronics engineer who was recently kidnapped—I think—from Connecticut, along with his most recent invention. It was some form of missile control, roughly the size of a walnut. That is all I know about it. Since I am not at the moment wearing a uniform, I am not permitted to know more than this."

"I have seen some reports concerning it," he said soberly. "You mean that the trail of the invention leads to Paris?"

"I think so. Know anything about Jason Chimique Société?"

"Yes," he said simply. "We have suspected them of dealing in certain military secrets, but we have never caught them."

"Them?"

He gave me a familiar smile. "All right, Milo. Him. Georges Piquet. He is the company. He is a mysterious man who comes and goes, and no one is quite sure where he goes and from whence he comes. He engages himself in various industrial chemical processes from which he makes much money. We believe that he does other things, but that is all."

"Did you ever hear of a Jason Johansson?"

He thought for a moment and then shook his head. "I do not know the name, Milo."

"I can't prove it at the moment," I said, "but I think that he and Piquet are the same."

"Who is Johansson?"

"He is a man who recently managed to get several industrial secrets in America, caused the deaths of at least four men, and, I think, kidnapped Angus Watson. He is also the owner of Jason Aktiebolag in Stockholm."

"You are sure?" he asked thoughtfully.

"Yes."

"We knew that Piquet's company leased many industrial patents from the Swedish company, but we did not know that there was any other connection. How did you learn of it?"

"Let's call it luck," I said with a smile. "Tell me, Henri, do you have a photograph of Piquet?"

"Of Piquet, yes. Of his face, no. When we first became interested in him, we took several photographs of him. But all we have are pictures of shoulders and arms and a hat. One could only assume that he objected to having his face photographed."

"The same thing is true of Johansson."

"Amusing," he said. "You have ideas?"

"Not really," I said. "Do you know an Andre Chaland?"

He smiled. "One of our more famous characters. He will do anything for a price."

"Why would he want to kill Piquet?"

He was thoughtful for a moment. "I didn't pay too much attention at the time, but I remember once hearing that he had killed someone for an important industrialist and had not been paid. Could that be the reason?"

"If I'm right, it could be. Do you know the place called Ma Petite?"

He laughed. "Milo, my friend, you are becoming forgetful. It is a place to which I took you once to meet a Russian girl.* I know it well, and it knows me well—but there they think that I am a big operator. Why do you ask?"

"I was attacked here in the hotel last night," I said. "The man who attacked me was killed a few hours later. There was a man in the next room who came to my rescue. He wishes me to have dinner with him tonight. I think I will do so and then later I will manage to excuse myself and go to Ma Petite."

"Why?"

"That is where Chaland told me to meet him. I think I would like to drop around once or twice before I have to contact him."

"I will meet you there," he said promptly.

"I don't know what time I can get away from this other man," I said.

He shrugged. "It makes no difference. I am not busy at the moment, so I will go there tonight, and when you come— there I am."

"All right."

"Now perhaps I should go," he said with a regretful look

---

* See *So Dead the Rose* by M.E. Chaber.

at the bottle of brandy. "It may be better if no one knows that there is a connection between us."

"I think so," I said. "There is one more thing you should know before we meet later tonight."

"What is that?"

"Chaland must have heard most of my conversation in the office and so will know that I work for an insurance company. It may hurt your standing in Ma Petite to be seen in the presence of an apparently honest businessman."

He smiled. "I'll fix that by spreading rumors about you before you arrive. Are you armed?"

I pulled up my trouser leg and showed him the gun strapped there. "It's not very heavy artillery, but it's good if the range isn't too far. I didn't want to try to smuggle in a larger gun."

"Wear it in a slightly more obvious place tonight. It doesn't have to be too obvious. They are very good there at spotting such things."

"All right. There is one more thing you can do for me. There is an American—or I think he's American—named Joseph Pitcher. He followed me in New York, but I beat him to an attack on me. Then I poured whiskey over him and called the cops. In the meantime, I called the police in Philadelphia, who were interested in him. I thought that would keep him out of action for a while, but he's here in Paris."

"You saw him?"

"I certainly did. He tried to run me down on the street with a Citroën today. See if you can find out where he's staying and anything else you can. I asked the police to check on him, but

I have no confidence in what they will get or tell me. I hate to bother you with this."

"*Allons donc!* I will go now."

"It's good to see you again, old friend," I said.

"*Chut!*" he said. "I will see you at Ma Petite." He waved his hand and was gone.

I poured another drink, and then there was a knock on the door. It was a waiter with my lunch. I ate it slowly, finishing my brandy, then decided I would take a nap since it was apt to be a long night. I undressed and went to sleep.

I was awakened by the telephone. I answered sleepily. It was Jean Nicot.

"Milo," he said, "is it possible for you to spend the evening with me, as I suggested in my message?"

"I can certainly have dinner with you," I said. "But I do have a late appointment and will have to leave after dinner."

"Ah, I understand," he said in a voice that only a Frenchman could use. It meant that he assumed I was meeting a woman—a beautiful woman, naturally. "I am not in the hotel and will not be able to return before we have dinner. Will you meet me at Le Cabaret two hours from now?"

"I'll be there," I said.

"Good. I will see you then." He hung up.

I came back to the world slowly and finally got out of bed. I looked at the bottle of brandy and decided it was too heavy for the time of day. I took a slow shower, shaved, and got dressed. I put the leg holster away and tucked the derringer under my belly where it wouldn't show too quickly. I went downstairs to the bar and ordered a martini and stayed there until it was time to leave for the meeting with Nicot.

I took a taxi in front of the hotel, and we had gone only a few blocks when I realized that somebody was following my cab. Whoever it was didn't make any special move, so I didn't worry too much about it. I was careful when I got out of the taxi in front of the restaurant, but the car following me had stopped a block away. I went inside, where Jean Nicot was already waiting at a table.

We had a fine dinner, including *blanquette de veau à l'ancienne* and a very good wine. This time we did not talk about the event of the night before, but about almost every subject we could think of. He was a charming man, and we had almost finished our coffee and brandy when I realized it was time to move on. I mentioned it, with apologies, but he was most understanding. He also insisted on paying the entire bill.

"I have my car here," he said as we left the restaurant. "May I drive you to your destination?"

I looked up the street and did not see the car that had followed me to the restaurant. "No, thanks," I said. "I think I'll walk off some of that excellent dinner and then take a taxi. I thank you, Jean, for an enjoyable evening. We must do it another time soon—on me."

"It was my pleasure, Milo. I wish you a wonderful evening." He gave me a jaunty wink and walked away. I watched him get into his Mercedes and drive off. I knew there was a taxi stand a couple of blocks down the street and I headed for it.

I had gone a block before it really registered. There were

footsteps behind me, footsteps that were matching mine almost perfectly. I was still being followed, this time on foot.

Instead of continuing ahead in the direction of the taxi stand, I turned to the right at the next street. I stopped, pushing my body up against the wall, and pulled the derringer from my belt. I kept lifting my feet up and down so that it would sound as if I were walking, and tried gradually to soften the sound so it would seem to be going farther away.

I could hear his steps. They slowed down and stopped altogether. Then there was a scuff of leather on concrete as he once again started moving carefully. He came around the corner, but stopped the minute he saw me.

It was Joe Pitcher. There was a gun in his hand. "Smart guy, huh?" he said. "You thought you had me bottled up with the cops. Now I'm going to make sure that you're buttoned up."

"So you are a button man?"

"Like I said, you're a smart guy."

"And Jason," I said, "hired you for a few executions in New York and then to finish with me?"

He hadn't yet spotted the small gun in my hand, which was my only advantage. But I didn't want to kill him; I wanted him alive to go back to face trial.

He laughed. "Sure. He got in touch with me again after some jerk he hired over here fell down on the job. Well, let's not waste any more time, smart guy."

TEN

He looked down the street to make sure there wasn't a witness. It didn't give me much time, but I decided to try. I had to lift my gun only slightly to bring it into line. Even so he caught some movement, for his head snapped back to face me.

"What the—" he began.

That was when I squeezed the trigger. I saw the little jump of cloth at his kneecap and knew I'd hit where I'd aimed. If I had any doubts, his strangled scream as he went down would have settled it. I moved forward quickly, and when he tried to lift his gun, I stepped on his hand. I leaned over and smashed my derringer against the point of his jaw. He subsided, unconscious.

There was still no one in sight. I tucked the derringer under my belt and swiftly crossed the street. I heard a window go up somewhere behind me.

"De quoi s'agit-il?" a voice called out.

"There has been an accident," I called back. "If you have a telephone, please call for an ambulance. I will go for a policeman." And I kept on going without waiting for an answer.

I reached the taxi stand and luckily there was a car there. I got in and told the driver to take me to Ma Petite.

It was a cellar place, and I suddenly remembered it as I went down the steps and stood in the doorway. The room was full of smoke, people, and scurrying waiters. A small combo was playing jazz and a beautiful black girl was singing. I looked around and finally spotted Henri Flambeau. He was sitting alone at a table against the wall. It was one of the few tables in the room that was not jammed up against other tables.

I made my way across the room, fending off waiters who wanted to lead me to a table. On the way, I glimpsed Chaland sitting in another spot. I gave a slight signal of recognition and continued on my way. I slipped into the chair opposite Henri.

"Welcome, my friend," he said. He nodded at a waiter, and a moment later there was a glass of brandy in front of me. Henri paused until the waiter was gone. "I have some news for you, Milo, but not yet enough."

"You didn't have much time," I admitted.

"Your Joseph Pitcher," he said, "there is no record of him entering France, so he must have entered with a false passport. I've started a search for him, but I don't know how long it will take to get results. In the meantime, I got a report on him from America. Do you want to hear it now?"

"Sure."

"His real name is Joseph Picci. He is a naturalized American citizen from Sicily. He is a known member of an organized crime syndicate, mostly known as a killer. He has a very long record, although he has spent very little time in prison. At the moment he is wanted very badly in your city of Philadelphia on suspicion of murder."

"Why didn't they grab him while the New York police had him?" I asked sourly.

He laughed. "It seems that your New York police are covered with chagrin. They thought they were merely arresting a drunk, so they were not too careful. He recovered consciousness while they were taking him in, hit one of the policemen, and took his gun. They are still looking for him. But we will soon find him, my friend."

"I know you will," I said with a smile. "I just left him."

"What?" he exclaimed. "Where?"

"On the street just around the corner from Le Cabaret."

"You killed him?"

"No. I want him to be extradited and tried. He expected to kill me, but he was careless. I shot him through the right kneecap, then knocked him out. Somebody in one of the buildings was curious, and I said there had been an accident and suggested that an ambulance be called while I went for the police. I came directly here. By this time he should be in some hospital and the object of a certain amount of police interest, since he was shot and his gun was on the sidewalk next to him."

"I see that time has not changed you, Milo," he said dryly. "Please excuse me while I take some steps to assure that he isn't treated as a tourist who happened to wander in front of a stray bullet."

"Don't mention me."

"Naturally not. I will be right back as soon as I have made a telephone call."

I watched him cross the room, saying hello to many persons at various tables, then start up the stairway. He obviously was not going to make the call from the club.

I sipped my brandy and waited. Suddenly I was aware that someone was standing beside the table. I looked up. It was Chaland.

"Pardon," he said. There was a touch of respect in his attitude, so I could guess that Henri had already spread his propaganda about me. "I did not realize that you were a friend of M'sieu Flambeau."

"There was no reason why you should realize it," I said coldly.

"True," he admitted. "I don't suppose you have yet learned anything?"

"No. And you?"

"Only that I am told that Piquet is definitely in Paris, no matter what is said. But I do not know where. He is not at his apartment or in any of the places he usually visits."

"We will find him," I said.

"I was not sure," he said hesitatingly, "if you had come to see me or not. Otherwise I would not have intruded."

Henri's rumor must have been a big one. "It is nothing," I said. "When I have something to tell you, I will come directly to see you."

"Of course, M'sieu," he said, and left.

Henri was back almost immediately. "It will be seen to," he said as he slipped into his chair.

I looked at him. "Henri, what did you say about me here?"

"Why?"

"Chaland came over to see me while you were gone and he was showing considerable respect. Why?"

He laughed. "I merely spread the word that I was meeting a

very important international operator and that I needed a special table so that our conversation could not be overheard. Their own imaginations supplied the rest. As soon as you entered and came to my table, one of the waiters went and talked to Chaland and was tipped. The same waiter also, I noticed, observed the gun under your belt. They have very sharp eyes for such things around here. Is that the gun you used tonight?"

"Yes. Perhaps I'd better do something about getting another one. I asked the police today to look into Joseph Pitcher and I am sure they will remember. Any ideas?"

He frowned. "I could get you one, but it might not be too intelligent. You can buy one here if you like. Of course, it will be stolen, so that you shouldn't keep it long."

"All right."

He beckoned to the waiter and whispered in his ear. The waiter nodded and left.

"I told him," Henri said, "that you would pay in dollars. You will get a better deal that way."

"Okay. How much?"

"Because you are a friend of mine," he said with a smile, "it will be a special price. It will cost you only fifty dollars, and that will include ammunition."

I took out fifty dollars and passed it to Henri. Holding it in his lap, he placed franc notes on top and underneath it, folded all of the money, and put it in his pocket.

The waiter returned with more brandy and a long loaf of bread wrapped loosely in an old newspaper. He placed it on the table between us, put the brandy in front of us, and accepted the money from Henri.

"It is inside the loaf of bread," Henri said when the waiter was gone. "It is hollowed out, and all you have to do is pull the two halves of the loaf apart. Tomorrow I will see what I can learn about Piquet. But there is one more thing, my friend ..."

"What is that?"

"I also learned today that there is no way that I can interfere officially in your problem. An order came through saying that you might be here but, if so, would be on civilian business. It added that we were to watch you but give you no assistance of any sort unless special permission was granted. I am sorry."

"That's the way it started back in the States," I told him.

"You understand, Milo, I will continue to do anything I can, but none of it will be official."

"I understand."

"Good. Now, perhaps, we—" He broke off. "Here comes a countryman of yours who is a bore. Don't be too friendly with him."

The man who was approaching the table was of medium height, walking with a slightly stooped gait. His hair and mustache were peppered black and white. He stopped at the table and looked at Henri.

"I hope I am not intruding," he said.

"Of course not," Henri said flatly, but he did not invite him to sit down.

"I haven't seen you in a couple of weeks," the man said. His gaze was going back and forth between Henri and me. His French bore a strong American accent.

"I've been busy," Henri said. He suddenly seemed aware of

the man's interest in me. "Oh, this is a compatriot of yours. M'sieu Milo March, M'sieu Doc Black."

So this was the man the detective had mentioned to me, I thought as he reached out to shake my hand.

"Hello," he said in English. "Glad to meet someone from back home."

"I imagine you are," I said.

"I see you are fond of the bread they make here at Ma Petite," he said, nodding toward the loaf on the table.

"Yes," I said.

There was a moment of awkward silence. Neither Henri nor I did anything to break it.

"Well," he said finally, going back to French, "it was nice meeting you. I will see you soon, Henri."

There was another moment of silence and he left.

"I am sorry, my friend," Henri said, "but there are some of your countrymen I cannot stand. I think there is something false about him."

"What does he do?" I asked.

Henri shrugged. "He is supposed to do a number of things, but the only thing I ever see is his women. Now, as I started to say, perhaps we should break up. I have work to do early in the morning so that I can spend some time trying to help you. Let us not leave together. Do you want to leave first or last?"

"I'd better leave first. It'll look less suspicious that way."

He nodded. "I will see you tomorrow, my friend."

I picked up my loaf of bread and left. I was aware that someone was coming up the stairs behind me, but I didn't look back. I reached the street and looked around. There were a couple of empty taxis in the next block, so I headed for them.

"Well," he said in English, "I didn't realize you were leaving at the same time as I was."

I looked around. It was Doc Black. There was something phony about his appearing just then. I didn't believe in coincidences.

"It's been a long day," I said curtly. "I decided I'd better get some sleep."

"I have a car. Can I drop you at your hotel?"

"No, thanks. I'll get a taxi. It'll be quicker."

"Sure," he said. "You know, I keep thinking that we have met before."

"I don't think so."

"I'm sure of it," he persisted. "I think we may have met here a few years ago. I remember that you had something to do with insurance. I suppose you're back here now on an interesting case, eh?"

Then I began to get it. I stopped and turned to face him. "Yes, I am," I said evenly. "A fascinating case. Did you ever hear of a man who called himself C. Jackson?"

His eyes shifted and I knew I had him. "I don't recall the name," he said.

"Sure you don't," I said in disgust. "You must be new in this game."

"New in this game?" he repeated. "I'm afraid I don't know what you mean."

"You will. Are you a betting man, Doc?"

"Well, I take a little flyer once in a while out at the track. Why?"

"Do you have a hundred dollars?"

"Yes." He looked puzzled.

"I'll make you a bet of one hundred dollars. We will go to the nearest public telephone and call Washington. I'll pay for the call. If General Sam Roberts never heard of you, you win my hundred dollars; if he knows you, I win your hundred dollars. Now, that's a fair bet, isn't it?"

"Well," he said nervously, "I don't mind betting on a horse now and then, but that seems like a pretty strange bet. I—I don't know this General you mentioned, but I don't think I'd like to make such a bet. You might have arranged it just to win the bet."

"Merde," I said. "In the meantime, you might check back on your orders. Unless the old bastard has changed his mind again, the orders are that you will not interfere with me, although it is also understood that you will give me only a minimum of cooperation. I accept this, but I don't want to have to be combing you out of my hair every few minutes. So get lost before you get hurt. This is a case that separates the men from the boys."

I turned and walked swiftly toward the taxis without waiting for a response. I gave the driver the name of my hotel and we took off—which is the only way to describe the way a French taxi driver begins driving.

When we reached the hotel, I went in and decided to stop at the bar for a last drink. There was brandy in my room, but I didn't feel like having any more of that. I went into the bar and took a seat and ordered a whiskey sour. It was only after I had given my order that I realized I was only two seats away from Jean Nicot. He spotted me at about the same time.

"Milo, my friend, I didn't expect to see you so early."

"It's not so early," I said, glancing at my watch. "It's one o'clock in the morning."

"One's appointments," he said, winking as only a Frenchman can, "may sometimes last all night. I trust that you were not disappointed."

"Not especially," I said. I didn't feel too much like talking, and apparently he didn't either, so we sat, drinking and exchanging occasional remarks, mostly about Paris. I had a second drink with him and we agreed to meet the following day. Then I went upstairs.

I took my loaf of bread apart, and there was a nice little Belgian automatic and two clips of bullets. It wasn't my idea of an ideal gun, but it would do. I tore the rest of the bread into small bits and flushed it down the toilet. I put one clip in the gun and then hid it, and the other clip where it wouldn't be found without a thorough search. I put away my derringer, undressed, and went to bed.

It was almost ten o'clock when I awakened the next morning. I had a small shot of brandy to get my eyes fully open, then took a shower and shaved. After that I called room service and ordered some breakfast and a bucket of ice.

The waiter arrived promptly. While he was arranging the table, I put some ice in a glass and poured brandy over it. The waiter saw what I was doing and shook his head, clucking to himself.

"M'sieu," he said, "brandy drinkers do not live long."

"I know," I said solemnly, "but look how much pleasure they have while they do live."

He shook his head again. I had the impression that he was about to rush out and light a candle for me.

"Attends," I said sternly. "Did you ever stop to 'wonder what the vintners buy one-half so precious as the goods they sell'?"*

His expression indicated that he had already given me up as a lost cause. "Perhaps, M'sieu, you are right," he said cautiously, "but I think that a good wine would be better."

"Brandy comes from a good wine," I said. "At least, I hope so."

"Of course, M'sieu," he said, resigned—and thinking of his tip. I paid him and he left. I settled down to my breakfast, including the brandy. In most European hotels you need the brandy first so that you can put up with the coffee.

I had finally worked my way down to coffee—reinforced with brandy so that I couldn't taste the chicory—when the phone rang. It was the hotel manager.

"I am sorry, M'sieu," he said, "but Detective Carot is on his way up to your room. He insisted."

"It is all right," I said. "I shall be happy to see Detective Carot."

I replaced the phone, finished the last of my coffee, and pushed the room-service table to one side, then made myself

---

* That is, what can the vintners buy that is as precious as the intoxication they sell? This is a couplet from the *Rubaiyat* of Omar Khayyam (Fitzgerald translation). The Persian poet speaks of how drinking has ruined his reputation, yet he cannot imagine anything more valuable than the happiness of drink.

a small brandy on the rocks. I had just finished when there was a knock on the door. I went over and opened it.

"Ah, Detective Carot," I exclaimed, "how nice to see you. Please come in." I waited until he was inside and I had closed the door. "I imagine that this means that you have some information?"

He sat down in a chair and looked at me with that same tired expression I had first observed on his face. "Perhaps," he said. He glanced around the room.

"You must forgive the appearance of my room," I said. "I haven't been awake very long. May I offer you a brandy?"

"No, thank you." He looked at my glass of brandy and, if anything, his expression became even more weary. "A little brandy is excellent for the health, but a steady consumption may be bad for the consumer. It is said that brandy drinkers do not live long."

I smiled at him. "I'm afraid you've been listening to too many waiters. In the meantime, it helps me to tolerate the coffee that is served here."

"Ah, you Americans," he exclaimed with a kind of Gallic superiority. "You asked me yesterday about the presence of an American named Joseph Pitcher who might be in Paris. Perhaps you recall?"

"I recall."

"I have found him."

"Marvelous," I said. "I did not expect such fast police work. Where is he?"

"His real name is Joseph Picci," he said heavily. "He did not, however, enter France under either name. He came here with a passport made out in the name of Peter Joseph." He lit a cigarette and looked at me over the tip of it. "Do you know a restaurant called Le Cabaret, M'sieu March?"

"Of course. I had dinner there last night."

"Exactly. Until what time were you there?"

"I believe I left shortly before eleven. You can easily check it. I had dinner with a M'sieu Jean Nicot, who is staying in this hotel. We left the restaurant together. He went to his car, and I took a taxi to Ma Petite and was there until about one o'clock. I then returned here to the hotel."

He sighed as if the weight of the world were on his shoulders. "I know," he said. "I have already talked to M'sieu Nicot, and he says approximately the same thing. But it leaves a certain curiosity unsatisfied."

"I'm a bit curious myself," I said. "If you would tell me what you're talking about, I might be able to give you more intelligent answers—if that's what you are looking for."

"It is a most unusual situation, M'sieu," he said. *"Attends.* Yesterday you came to see me concerning cooperation about information. Among other things, you asked about a man who called himself Joseph Pitcher. Very good. Shortly after eleven last night a gunshot was heard one block from Le Cabaret. The householder who heard the shot opened his window and inquired as to what was happening. He has testified that a man, whom he could not see clearly enough to identify, shouted that there had been an accident and asked him to telephone for an ambulance. He also testified that the man said he was going for the police, although he did not do so."

"That is very interesting," I said, "but I fail to see what it has to do with me."

"We will come to that, M'sieu. Shortly before twelve o'clock last night, we, the police, received a telephone call from a government official telling us that we might be interested in a man who had been picked up by an ambulance on the street. Before we could investigate, a report came in from the Saint Peter's Hospital that they had a man who had been wounded by a gunshot and that the man carried an American passport and also had apparently been carrying a gun. The man turned out to be the man you were interested in. He was identified through his fingerprints."

"Was he seriously injured?" I asked gravely.

He gave me a sour look. "He was shot through the right kneecap and was hit on the jaw by a metal object. The bullet that hit him was a .32 caliber, but the markings on the bullet are not similar to those of any known make. Do you own such a gun, M'sieu?"

"We've already gone through that," I said. "Do you see any sort of gun on me? Do you see any sort of gun in my room?"

"No, but I have not looked everywhere. I could easily get an order to do so."

"Go ahead. Be my guest."

"I do not understand you, M'sieu," he said heavily. "You come into my office and say that you wish to cooperate. But when I look back on our conversation, I find that you have really told me nothing. You have told me what work I should do and that I should share the results with you, and that is all. Then a man in whom you are interested gets shot in a neighborhood where you have been dining. As an alibi, you claim that you were already at a club that is known as a favorite spot of many French criminals."

"Why don't you ask the wounded man who shot him?"

"We did. He refuses to say. And this morning your country applied to have him extradited on a charge of murder."

"So what is this all about?"

"We do not like shootings in France, M'sieu, even if the victim is a known criminal."

"Of course you don't like shootings," I said, "but you don't mind the police running around and hitting people with lead-filled capes."*

"M'sieu March," he said sadly, "that is hitting below the belt."

"But not with a cape lined with lead," I reminded him. "I also don't like shootings—in France or elsewhere. I am also not the place for you to deposit all of your troubles. I am not a gangster. I am a perfectly legitimate businessman who is here in your country on perfectly legitimate business. Either accept me as such or tell me that I am under arrest and I will call my embassy."

He sighed heavily. "This is what you call cooperation?"

"I don't have any information to share. When I have it, I will share it. But I am unlikely ever to have any if you insist on taking up all of my time asking foolish questions."

---

* The French police in cities began wearing capes (called *pèlerines*) early in the 20th century and stopped wearing them in 1967 (two years after this book was published). The seams were lined with lead, possibly to weight the capes so that they would hang properly, but the policemen would roll up the cape and use it to beat people.

"Very well, M'sieu," he said with offended dignity. He stood up. "I will see you again."

"Don't hurry," I said.

He gave me a hurt look and left.

I closed the door and went back to the bed. Something was bothering me and I didn't know what it was. I knew that somewhere in the case there was something that was out of focus. But what?

I looked at the bottle of brandy and decided that maybe the waiters knew what they were talking about. I called downstairs and asked room service to send me a pitcher of dry martinis. This resulted in some conversation about what was a pitcher, but we finally got it settled.

The waiter arrived with the order, and it was more of a pitcher than I had anticipated. It must have held about eight martinis. The waiter had such an admiring look that I paid for it as if that were my usual order.

I poured a drink and took a taste. It was good. I leaned back and started thinking about what had happened since I had left the States. Then there was a knock on the door. This time I stopped before opening it and took one of my guns from the drawer. It was Henri Flambeau.

"Come in, my friend," I said. "You are just in time."

"For what?" he asked, coming in.

"I ordered a pitcher of martinis and I think they sent a magnum."

"I'm always ready to serve the cause of friendship," he said solemnly.

I poured a martini for him and went back to stretch out in

my favorite position on the bed. "I have one piece of information for you. You have a brother at Ma Petite."

"Oh?"

"Doc Black," I said. "He works for General Roberts in Washington."

He looked surprised. "You're sure?"

"Positive. He followed me out of Ma Petite last night and tried to find out what was going on. I offered to make a bet with him and pay for a phone call to General Roberts. He chickened out."

"Oh, well," he said with a shrug, "those things do happen in this business. I should have listened to my mother. She wanted me to be a baker."

"You should have listened to her," I said gravely. "Do you have any information for me?"

"Nothing of importance. The request for the extradition of Joseph Picci has already been made and will, of course, be granted. He has refused to make any statement about his reason for being here or who shot him."

"I know. Detective Carot has already been here wanting to know if I possess a gun that might have been used in the shooting. I'm afraid I was a little rough with him."

"But he did not search your room?"

"No. He may change his mind at any moment."

"True. Are you making any progress, my friend?"

"I think I'm about to. There is something wrong in the picture, but I haven't yet uncovered it. In the meantime, I would like to put you to work."

"Doing what?"

"When Johansson, or Piquet, was recently working in America, there were four men who either committed suicide or were murdered. There was another man who simply disappeared, Angus Watson. He is the one most related to your kind of work. He invented the missile control. The invention disappeared with him, but there is still his brain. If a man wanted to sell the invention behind the Iron Curtain, he might think he would get a higher price if he could deliver both the brain and the invention."

"You have something in mind?" he asked, his eyes bright with interest.

"Let us sum up," I said. "There was a man recently in America who called himself C. Jackson, Carl Johnson, or Calvin Johns. There is no question that this man was also one Jason Johansson, the owner of Jason Aktiebolag in Stockholm. There is no question in my mind about this. And it was as C. Jackson that he contacted Angus Watson, who was never seen again after their meeting."

"We," he said cheerfully, "do not know that connection, but I have no doubt that you are correct. I have worked with you too often to think otherwise. But you are getting at something, my friend. What?"

"Jason Johansson arrived back in Sweden after some considerable absence and stayed only a few days. But he did not arrive alone. There was a 'sick gentleman' with him, according to the woman who cares for his house. A very sick gentleman."

"You think that was Watson?"

"I do. Now we move to a man named Piquet, who is the

owner of a French corporation that does much business with the Swedish corporation. M'sieu Piquet also spends much time abroad. He returned to France at about the time that Herr Johansson left Sweden. M'sieu Piquet also arrived home accompanied by a sick friend—one who was so ill that he was in a wheelchair and under such heavy sedation that Piquet had to give all of his answers to the customs officials."

"Where did you learn this?" he exclaimed.

"From the police."

"You are right. It is too much of a coincidence."

"The police," I continued, "believe that Piquet has left France for West Germany. I do not believe this. I think he is still in Paris. A man who has five names can just as easily have six or seven. And I believe that Angus Watson is somewhere in Paris, but may not be for long. I think he is destined for another city. Where?"

"Moscow," he said promptly. "The price would be too high for anyone else."

"Exactly. I will find Piquet. I want you to find Angus Watson. You can do it more easily than I can."

He finished his martini and literally leaped to his feet. "I will do it at once. You are a genius, my friend."

He was out of the door before I could say anything. But I had no doubt that he would do what I had asked.

I went back to the bed and poured myself another martini. I sipped it slowly and began to think, searching for whatever it was that was wrong. I carefully went over everything that had happened since I had arrived in Paris. I knew that there was something I had overlooked that was important, and it was only a question of finding it.

Then, suddenly, I thought I had it. I made sure that I was presentable and went downstairs to see the manager.

"M'sieu," I said, "I do not want to intrude on anything that might be personal, but I would like to ask you a question."

"Yes?" he asked.

"As you know, I have become somewhat friendly with M'sieu Jean Nicot, who is in the room next to mine, since he came to my aid the other night. I wonder if you could tell me when M'sieu Nicot checked into the hotel."

"I see no harm in that," he said. "Permit me to look at the records." He got out his cards and shuffled through them. Finally he looked up. "He checked in the same night that you did."

"Before or afterwards?"

He consulted the card again. "Shortly afterwards. Fifteen minutes, according to the record."

"Merci," I said. "Could you tell me if M'sieu Nicot comes here often?"

"This is his first time," he said.

"I thank you again. ... Oh, yes, M'sieu, this is not a secret matter. You may feel perfectly free to tell M'sieu Nicot what I asked you. I would have asked him personally if he had been around."

"Of course, M'sieu," he said solemnly.

I thanked him again and went back upstairs. I poured another martini and thought some more as I drank it. It only made me certain that I was right. I got up and put my derringer on top of the dresser. The small Belgian automatic I put under the pillow on my bed. Then I got undressed and climbed into bed.

All I had to do was wait—so I went to sleep.

ELEVEN

The evening was well upon us when I awakened. I got up
and took a shower, then put on a pair of shorts and stretched
out on the bed again. I lit a cigarette and checked the martini
pitcher. It was still half full. I picked up the phone and
ordered some dinner from room service. I also asked them
to send up a newspaper and a copy of *Paris Match*. I went
over and unlocked the door, then went back to the bed to
wait. Waiting is a large part of my business, so I have developed a talent for it.

My ice had not entirely melted, and I poured a martini on
the rocks. It wasn't long before there was a knock on the door.
I called out that the door was not locked. The waiter came in,
pushing the table ahead of him. He placed it beside the bed
and uncovered the dishes with a flourish. He put the newspaper and the magazine beside the plate and looked at me for
approval. I gave it in the form of cash, and he left.

The dinner was excellent, and the news was about the
same as I might have read back in New York. I was halfway
through both when the phone rang. I answered. It was Henri
Flambeau.

"Milo," he said, "I am downstairs. May I come up?"
"Yes."

It took him only a few minutes. He knocked and came in

when I called out. I offered him a choice of the remaining martini or some brandy. He chose the latter and I poured it for him.

"You are relaxed, I see," he said.

"Why not?" I asked. "There comes a time in every case when there is nothing to do but wait."

"You have solved the case?"

"Part of it. In my mind. But it won't be solved until Piquet makes a move. He will, and then that part will be solved."

"I have some news," he said, "but not too much. I located the taxi driver who picked up Piquet and his invalid friend when they arrived in Paris. Guess where he took them."

"An embassy?"

"Close. He let them out a block away from the Russian embassy. The last the driver saw of them, Piquet was pushing his friend in the wheelchair down the street. I also discovered that the police have been trying to find Piquet's friend with no success. He is not registered anywhere."

"I expected that. What do you think, Henri?"

"I think your missing inventor is at the Russian embassy. That does not make it easy, my friend."

"It's never easy. Do you think they're going to keep him there?"

"I have a wild idea," he said. "The embassy has given notice that it is shipping a boxful of official papers back to Moscow tomorrow morning. Since they are diplomatic papers, they will not be examined. The box, by some miracle, is large enough to contain a person."

"An interesting thought," I said. "Is that all?"

"Well, unofficially I can tell you that I heard that the embassy chauffeur will leave the embassy at nine o'clock in the morning to deliver the box to the airport." He smiled at me. "This is an area in which I cannot help you, my friend. We will meet again."

He stood up and walked rapidly from the room.

I finished my dinner, thinking about it. I remembered that not long ago there had been an attempt at smuggling a man out of France in a box, so maybe it made sense. And Henri was a smart operator who had made few mistakes in the many years I had known him.

I put on my pants, a shirt, and a pair of shoes, and went downstairs. The manager was gone, but the assistant manager was on duty. So I saw him.

"I am sorry to bother you, M'sieu," I said, "but I need some special service."

"Anything we can do will be a pleasure, M'sieu."

"I want to rent a car and I want it to be here at the hotel not later than nine o'clock tomorrow morning. But I want a special car. I want an old Citroën, one of the big ones. Do you think it could be arranged?"

He hesitated. "Well, it doesn't give us much time, but I believe there is a place where we can secure one. Of course, there would have to be a deposit."

"I will deposit the full amount that the car is worth the minute you can tell me it will be here."

That made up his mind for him. He reached for the telephone and made a call. A couple of minutes later he hung up and told me the car would be there promptly at nine in the morning. He also told me the value of the car, took down the number of my international driver's license, and accepted money from me.

On the way back to my room I stopped at the desk and asked the clerk if Jean Nicot had returned. He had not. I told the clerk to inform M'sieu Nicot, when he did come in, that I had asked about him and had been concerned for his welfare. Then I continued on to my room.

I undressed once more, poured myself a brandy, and got on the bed again. I felt lousy; in fact, I felt like getting drunk. I always feel that way when I know how a case is going to end. But I knew it was a luxury I couldn't afford at that moment, so I sipped sparingly on the brandy and read *Match*. It was an interesting issue, but I found it difficult to concentrate on what I was reading.

The time passed slowly, but there was no way that I could speed it up. I read some of the articles twice and looked at the pictures of the pretty girls several times. I had another brandy, but it didn't alleviate my tension. Maybe, I thought, I had been wrong. ...

Then, suddenly, shortly after midnight, there was a soft knock on my door. As soon as I heard it, I felt all right. I relaxed, lying on my side with my arm under the pillow.

"Come in," I called.

The door opened and Jean Nicot came in, closing the door behind him.

"I am sorry to intrude, Milo," he said with a smile. He looked around the room, then his gaze came back to me. "They told me at the desk that you had asked for me, and I thought it was something very important."

"Not in that sense," I said. "I decided not to go out tonight, and I guess I was lonely. Help yourself to a brandy and sit down for a few minutes."

He poured himself a brandy and went to a chair. He hesitated a moment, staring at the derringer on the dresser, then sat down. He lifted the glass.

"Your health, Milo," he said.

"And your health, Jean," I responded. "I also wanted to see you because I owe you so much."

"You owe nothing," he murmured. "It was merely lucky that I was present. Anyone would have done the same."

"I owe you more than that," I said. "If it weren't for you, I wouldn't be here. And I wanted to express my feelings about it before I left Paris."

"You are leaving?"

"Tomorrow. I have accomplished what I came here to do, and it is time that I return home. There remain only one or two small details, so I should be off early tomorrow."

He lifted his glass again. "I will miss you, Milo," he said. He drank and put the glass down. He took the handkerchief from his breast pocket, pressed it to his lips, then reached inside his coat and came out with a gun.

"I will miss you, Milo," he said. "You are an adversary to be admired."

"Flattery will get you nowhere," I told him. "I know that you are C. Jackson, Carl Johnson, Calvin Johns, Jason Johansson, George Piquet, and Jean Nicot. How did you know that I was looking for you?"

The gun in his right hand was steady as he reached with

his left hand for the glass and took a drink. "An excellent brandy," he said with a smile. "It was really careless of you to put your gun on the dresser. Is that the one you used to shoot poor Joseph Picci?"

"Yes. But you haven't answered my question."

"I knew about you, my dear boy," he said, "before I even went to America. I am very familiar with insurance, and whenever I embark on an endeavor, I make a careful study of the insurance company or companies involved and who they depend upon to solve their cases. I had a healthy respect for you before I even went to America. I know that I did not overestimate you; my only advantage was that I was always one step ahead of you."

"Well, sometimes that's the way it goes," I said.

"Since your gun is on the dresser," he said, "tell me how you knew that Jean Nicot was the man you were looking for?"

"Cases are funny," I told him. "Most of the time the man I'm looking for trips himself up. In a way, that is true of you. I had some luck in tracing you to Paris, but it was here that you overplayed your hand by being too anxious to know what I was doing."

"I don't understand."

"Of course you don't. Let's take it step by step. First, although you claimed that you make regular business trips to Paris, this is the first time you have ever stayed at this hotel. And you checked in about fifteen minutes after I did."

"Yes, I was informed you had asked about the time I checked in here. Go on."

"Then there was the attack on me that night. No one knew

where I was going to stay. Also, I do not think the attack was genuine. I was careless when I opened the door because I was expecting a hotel employee. If he'd really meant to kill me, he would have had the knife in me before I knew what was happening. And you showed up to the rescue very conveniently, then fussed over me like a mother hen until he could escape. It finally dawned on me that the whole thing was arranged so that you could meet me under circumstances that would make you seem friendly to me."

"Very good reasoning," he said, nodding.

"The man who pretended to attack me was found murdered the next morning. You had him killed, didn't you, so that he couldn't identify you?"

"It is an efficient method."

"Of course. Then there was the case of your friend Joseph Pitcher, or Joseph Picci, who made two attempts on me—not counting the one in New York. Someone had to tell him where I was staying, or he couldn't have followed me when he tried to run me down on the street. Then last night I was having dinner with you just before he made his second attempt."

"And poor Joseph failed," he said. "It isn't often that he does. I am curious about something. Why did you not kill him? I presume that you shot him where you intended to and it was not an accident that you hit him in the knee."

"I wanted him alive so he can testify against you."

"He will never testify against me," he said firmly.

"He will. I promise you."

He smiled. "M'sieu March, you are very clever or you would never have followed me this far, but you rate yourself too high. Joseph will not testify against me because by tomorrow night he will be dead. You will not be able to prevent this, since, unfortunately, you will not then be alive yourself. I assure you, M'sieu, that I regret this. I have formed a fondness for you, and I also possess a certain admiration for you—the only man who has ever come near to ruining my way of life. But it is necessary."

"You touch me deeply," I said dryly. "You do have an interesting theory. You seem to believe that all you have to do is kill off everyone who has worked with you or for you or has known what you do, and in that way you will never be caught."

"It has worked very well for ten years. I see no reason why it should not continue to do so for another ten years. By then I should be worth fifty million dollars and be ready to retire."

"You can be traced through your companies, you know. To some degree that is what I did."

"Yes, I know. Companies can also be killed. As a matter of fact, my friend, I have just tonight completed arrangements to sell my French and my Swedish interests. There will be new companies."

"The people in those companies with whom you worked will be able to identify you."

"They, too, will vanish."

"What about Angus Watson?" I asked. "He saw you. Did you also kill him?"

"One does not kill something that is extremely valuable. But you may be sure that he will never appear against me."

"Everything is neatly worked out," I said. Suddenly I felt

tired. "Do you object if I have a cigarette and some of my brandy?"

"Of course not," he said promptly. "Your cigarettes and brandy are right next to the bed. Reach out and help yourself. As long as you are there and your gun is here on the dresser, that is fine. Since you are wearing nothing but shorts, you cannot have any concealed weapons—except possibly for the ladies." He laughed heartily at his own joke.

I reached with my left hand for a cigarette and then for my lighter. When the cigarette was burning, I put it in the ashtray and picked up my glass of brandy. The feel of the brandy in my throat was a relief.

"Why didn't you kill me as soon as you walked in?" I asked.

He shrugged. "There is no hurry. Who will stop me? It is already late at night, and the sound of the shot will mean nothing, even if someone hears it. Besides, as I told you, I am fond of you."

"Oh, yes, I forgot that, didn't I? You know, you are all exactly alike."

"What do you mean?"

"Criminals," I said. "You live on inflated egos. No matter what happens, you think that you are smarter than anyone else. Others may get careless or make mistakes, but you think you won't. That's what is really funny about all of you—from hubcap thieves to you so-called international swindlers."

His face darkened with anger. "What are you talking about?" he asked harshly.

"I could make a whole list of the times you've been care-less, from the time you made a phone call in Connecticut from your hotel to a public phone at a gas station, right up until tonight."

"Tonight?"

"Tonight," I repeated firmly. "You've been talking a lot about how careless I was in leaving my gun on the dresser, but I haven't heard you say anything about being careless yourself."

"In what way?" he asked. He was still angry and the gun was held steadily on me.

I put my cigarette down and took another drink of brandy. I picked up the cigarette and drew on it.

"You saw the gun on the dresser and that answered all of your questions. You started out by thinking that I am stupid. You didn't think of checking the rest of the room or the closet." I hesitated while I concentrated on my cigarette for a second. "You didn't even think of checking the bathroom."

That was the one that stopped him. He hesitated, the gun wavering. But I had presented him with a compulsion that he could not resist. He looked at the bathroom.

When his gaze shifted back to me, I already had the Belgian automatic out, and there had been plenty of time to sight on the target. His eyes widened as he saw it.

"You were careless again," I said, and pulled the trigger.

The bullet struck just above the point where his jacket was buttoned. His white shirt twitched and suddenly became red. A look of disbelief spread over his face even as he was falling off the chair. The tendons in his hand stood out as he tried to pull the trigger of his gun, but he couldn't quite make it. He hit the floor with a thud, the gun bouncing out of his hand. The chair fell immediately after he did.

I waited a minute because you can never tell about small-caliber guns. His body twitched a couple of times but that was all. I got out of bed and walked over to look at him. I couldn't see any signs of life. I put my automatic down on the dresser and thought about the situation for a minute. It was not the ideal end, but it was better than if I were the one lying on the floor.

It was one-thirty in the morning. I put on a pair of pants, a shirt, and my shoes. I tucked the automatic in my pocket. Then I bent over the body on the floor and looked through his pockets until I found the key to his door. I had just straightened up with it when the phone rang. I picked it up and answered.

"M'sieu," a voice said apologetically, "this is the clerk. I am sorry to disturb you, but a tenant has claimed that he thought he heard a gunshot from your room."

I gave an embarrassed laugh. "I am terribly sorry, M'sieu," I said. "I am planning a trip through France in the morning—I have already rented a car through the hotel—and I was getting my camera equipment ready. I'm afraid that I dropped a flashbulb. Please extend my apologies to the tenant. It will not happen again."

"Very well, M'sieu," he said patiently. He hung up.

I lit a fresh cigarette and waited ten minutes. Then I opened my door and checked the corridor. It was empty, and there were no sounds from any of the rooms. I stepped out and unlocked the door to the next room. I put the key in my pocket and went back to my own room.

I put my hands under the arms of Jean Nicot, or whatever his name was, and dragged him to the door.

Once more I checked the corridor. It was empty. I dragged Nicot out of my room and into his, closing the door behind us. I arranged him tastefully on the floor not far from the bed. I went back to my own room and used my pen to pick up his gun, thrusting it through the trigger guard. I looked outside again, then returned to his room. I placed his gun near his body. I took out my automatic, used my handkerchief to remove any fingerprints that might be on it, and put it on the floor next to the bed.

Deciding I might as well be artistic, I mussed up the bed. The French love to think that many crimes are ones of passion. I didn't want to disillusion them. I mussed up Nicot's clothing. Then I looked through his things and found a bottle of heavily scented cologne. I sprinkled some of it over the bed and replaced the bottle in his case. I put his key back in his pocket, snapped the lock on his door, and then used my handkerchief to remove any prints that might be on the doorknob.

I went back to my room. I checked everything in it. There wasn't anything out of order. I had a final drink of brandy, put my derringer out of sight, and went to sleep.

At eight o'clock I was awake. While it was dangerous, I had already decided it would be too suspicious if I checked out, so I dressed, put everything that was important in my pockets, and went downstairs. I had a fast breakfast, and by eight-thirty I was behind the wheel of my rented Citroën. A few minutes later I was parked not far from the Russian embassy. I lit a cigarette and waited.

It was exactly nine o'clock when a Mercedes-Benz limousine pulled out of the embassy and started down the street. There was a uniformed chauffeur behind the wheel and some sort of box in the rear. Praying that I was right, I swung out into the street and followed him.

If he was heading for the airport, my best chance would be in the first few blocks, because we were on a quiet street. Once we hit the business sections of Paris, I wouldn't have a chance. So I made my move when we were about three blocks from the embassy. I gunned the motor and started to pass him. Then, just as I was even with his car, I swung sharply to the left. The two cars clashed with a shrieking of metal, and the Mercedes went up on the sidewalk and hit a tree.

I was out of my car almost before it stopped, shouting at the chauffeur in French. He wasn't hurt, but he was dazed as he climbed out of the car, trying to protest in very bad French, meanwhile pointing at the diplomatic license plates on his car.

There was no reason for wasting time. As soon as I was within reach, I hit him as hard as I could. He went down and was out. I grabbed a tire tool from my car and opened the back door of the Mercedes. I went to work on the box and quickly pried off one side.

Then I breathed a sigh of relief. There was a man inside. He was all doubled up and completely unconscious, but he had a faint pulse, so he was probably only drugged. I pulled him out of the box and carried him to my car, putting him flat on the rear seat. He looked like the description of Angus Watson.

When I had pulled him from the box, I noticed a small package that was placed between his feet. I went back and got it. I shook it and something rattled inside. I took it with me back to the Citroen. The left front fender was badly crumpled, but that seemed to be the only damage.

Two people had appeared on the street, and the chauffeur was beginning to twitch as I slid behind the wheel. I started the motor and took the Citroën out of there as fast as I could.

Even as I was driving, I was thinking about the situation. I decided then that it was a mistake for me to try to get Watson back to America on my own. I switched routes and a few minutes later arrived at the American embassy. I parked on the side street, where I hoped the car wouldn't be noticed. I put the package in my pocket, picked up Angus Watson, and carried him to the embassy.

Inside, I placed him on a sort of couch and then looked at the startled receptionist. "Get me somebody," I said, "but not just anybody. There is not much time."

I have to give her credit for one thing. She didn't ask any questions but got right on the phone. And a minute later there was a well-dressed young man at my elbow.

"I am the ambassador's secretary," he said, ignoring the limp body beside me. "May I help you?"

"You'd better," I said grimly.

I had my identification, including my passport, out, and I shoved it into his hands.

"I don't have much time, so listen carefully the first time. This man is an American named Angus Watson. He is very important to the security people in the States, where he was kidnapped sometime ago. I suggest that you check with General Sam Roberts in Washington as quickly as you can."

He nodded at the receptionist, and she was on the phone immediately.

I took the package from my pocket. "I think," I said, "that this is also something which they are very interested in back home, something that Angus Watson invented. It has such a top security rating that I wouldn't look at it, if I were you."

He accepted it gingerly, as though he were afraid it would go off in his hands. "This is most unusual, Mr.—er—March. Where did you find this gentleman and what is wrong with him?"

"For the moment let us merely say that he was in the possession of another government and was about to be shipped out of France to the home country of that other government. He is heavily drugged, but I imagine he will be all right once he comes out of it."

"I see," he said in a tone of voice that indicated he didn't see at all. "How did you happen to get—er—custody of him?"

"It's better if we don't talk about that at the moment. It might be embarrassing to you."

Just then the girl made a noise in her throat and he went to the phone. He made sure that he was speaking to General Roberts and then mentioned my name and that of Angus Watson, and gave a brief but somewhat incoherent version of what was happening. Then he merely began to make noises of agreement.

That was all I wanted to know. I eased over to the desk and took my identification from his hands.

He grunted another assent into the phone, then covered the mouthpiece with his hand. "The General wants to talk to you," he said.

"Not now," I told him. "Tell the General that the signal is red and that I will make a complete report as soon as I get back." I headed for the door.

"But—" he started to say, but I was outside and had closed the door before I could hear any more.

I got into the car and drove about four blocks and parked it. I used my handkerchief to remove any fingerprints I might have left on it. Then I found a taxi and told the driver what I wanted. A few minutes later he stopped in front of a cluster of secondhand stores. I had him wait while I went shopping. I bought a good, but old, suitcase, and then I bought enough used clothes to fill it. I went back to the driver and told him to take me to the airport.

I was in luck. There was a plane leaving for Denmark in a few minutes, and there was a seat available. I bought a ticket and then went through customs. There was no problem and it did not take long, since I was leaving instead of arriving.

I was waiting to board the plane when I heard my name called. I looked around, and there, a few feet away, was Chaland, the little character from Ma Petite.

"M'sieu," he said reproachfully, "you are leaving without coming to see me?"

"It would seem so," I said, "but I assure you that the reason is one of the utmost urgency."

"And what of our agreement?"

"You should be able to read about it in the newspaper later today or tomorrow morning. I believe that it will please you. In the meantime, I would not linger if I were you."

"Ah, I understand," he said. "Good luck, M'sieu." He

vanished, lost somewhere in the groups of people waiting for planes.

I boarded the plane but didn't take an easy breath until the door closed. The plane began to taxi down the runway, and I was looking out the window when I saw something that made me smile happily. I got a swift glimpse of Detective Maurice Carot running toward the loading gate, waving his arms.

I knew he couldn't see me, but I waved back.

TWELVE

It was nice and quiet when I finally came down on the field in Stockholm. I checked through the officials, got some local money, and went to a phone. First I put in a call to Henri Flambeau in Paris. It took a little maneuvering, but I finally got through to him without saying too much.

"Is it safe to talk?" I asked when he finally came on.

"I think so," he said. "We check these phones every few days. Where are you?"

"Stockholm."

"Good," he said. "Don't come back too quickly. You're not exactly popular in certain quarters."

"Johansson?"

"Well, that's one reason. There's no direct connection, but they are a little curious about you leaving so suddenly and not taking your clothes with you. There's one thing about it which may make you feel better."

"It'd better be good."

"Johansson is still alive. He's not in very good shape, and he'll be in the hospital for some time, but he'll recover, so he can be extradited."

"Has he said who shot him?"

"He's refused to talk about anything, but there is a certain amount of suspicion—and not only in that one direction."

"Oh, that!"

He laughed. "You did a great job, Milo. And a certain embassy is raising hell. The chauffeur gave a pretty accurate description of you, and they found the car you rented with damages that correspond to the accident. The only good thing is that they cannot tell what really happened. I gather that my guess about the box was correct?"

"Completely."

"I won't ask details, but I assume your compatriot is safe?"

"On American ground," I said.

"I understand. There will probably be some fuss made about this after you get back, but I wouldn't worry too much about it. They don't have enough to be sure of their charges. Take a short vacation and it'll probably blow over by then."

"Sounds like a good idea. Well, I just wanted to check. Are the wheels of justice in motion concerning Johansson?"

"I am told so. Anyway, it's out of your hands now. Only the next time, don't leave so suddenly. We had no chance to have an evening of pleasure together."

"Next time," I said. "Take care, Henri."

"You, too, my friend."

I hung up and went to the cablegram office. I sent two cables. The first went to General Sam Roberts in Washington. It said:

CHESTNUTS ARE NOW OUT OF THE FIRE. UP TO YOU TO GET THEM OUT OF THE COUNTRY. LOVES AND KISSES TO ALL YOUR BOYS.

MILO

The other one went to Martin Raymond at Intercontinental. It was just as short:

REASSURE THE BOARD OF DIRECTORS. I STILL HAVE SOME EXPENSE MONEY LEFT SO AM TAKING A VACATION.

MILO

As soon as they were sent, I went back to the phone and called Kerstin. She answered on the second ring.

"This is Milo," I said. "Are you busy?"

"I wasn't," she said, "but I expect to be now."

"You're damned right," I said. "Meet me at the restaurant. We're about to start a week's vacation."

"Wow!" she said—or the Swedish equivalent of it.

You know something? She used exactly the right word for that vacation.

ABOUT THE AUTHOR

Kendell Foster Crossen
(1910–1981), the only child
of Samuel Richard Cros-
sen and Clo Foster Cros-
sen, was born on a farm
outside Albany in Athens
County, Ohio—a village of
some 550 souls in the year
of this birth. His ancestors
on his mother's side include
the 19th-century songwriter
Stephen Collins Foster
("Oh! Susanna"); William
Allen, founder of Allentown, Pennsylvania; and Ebenezer
Foster, one of the Minute Men who sprang to arms at the
Lexington alarm in April 1775.

Ken went to Rio Grande College on a football scholarship
but stayed only one year. "When I was fairly young, I developed the disgusting habit of reading," says Milo March,
and it seems Ken Crossen, too, preferred self-education.
He loved literature and poetry; favorite authors included
Christopher Marlowe and Robert Service. He also enjoyed
participant sports and was a semi-pro fighter in the heavy-

weight class. He became a practicing magician and had a passion for chess.

After college Ken wrote several one-act plays that were produced in a small Cleveland theater. He worked in steel mills and Fisher Body plants. Then he was employed as an insurance investigator, or "claims adjuster," in Cleveland. But he left the job and returned to the theater, now as a performer: a tumbling clown in the Tom Mix Circus; a comic and carnival barker for a tent show, and an actor in a medicine show.

In 1935, Ken hitchhiked to New York City with a typewriter under his arm, and found work with the WPA Writers' Project, covering cricket for the *New York City Guidebook.* In 1936, he was hired by the Munsey Publishing Company as associate editor of the popular *Detective Fiction Weekly.* The company asked him to come up with a character to compete with The Shadow, and thus was born a unique superhero of pulps, comic books, and radio—The Green Lama, an American mystic trained in Tibetan Buddhism.

Crossen sold his first story, "The Aaron Burr Murder Case," to *Detective Fiction Weekly* in September 1939, but says he didn't begin to make a living from writing till 1941. He tried his hand at publishing true crime magazines, comics, and a picture magazine, without great success, so he set out for Hollywood. From his typewriter flowed hundreds of stories, short novels for magazines, scripts radio, television, and film, nonfiction articles. He delved into science fiction in the 1950s, starting with "Restricted Clientele" (February 1951). His dystopian novels *Year of Consent* and *The Rest Must Die* also appeared in this decade.

In the course of his career Ken Crossen acquired six pseudonyms: Richard Foster, Bennett Barlay, Kent Richards, Clay Richards, Christopher Monig, and M.E. Chaber. The variety was necessary because different publishers wanted to reserve specific bylines for their own publications. Ken based "M.E. Chaber" on the Hebrew word for "author," *mechaber.*

In the early '50s, as M.E. Chaber, Crossen began to write a series of full-length mystery/espionage novels featuring Milo March, an insurance investigator. The first, *Hangman's Harvest,* was published in 1952. In all, there are twenty-two Milo March novels. One, *The Man Inside,* was made into a British film starring Jack Palance.

Most of Ken's characters were private detectives, and Milo was the most popular. Paperback Library reissued twenty-five Crossen titles in 1970–1971, with covers by Robert McGinnis. Twenty were Milo March novels, four featured an insurance investigator named Brian Brett, and one was about CIA agent Kim Locke.

Crossen excelled at producing well-plotted entertainment with fast-moving action. His research skills were a strong asset, back when research meant long hours searching library microfilms and poring over street maps and hotel floorplans. His imagination took him to many international hot spots, although he himself never traveled abroad. Like Milo March, he hated flying ("When you've seen one cloud, you've seen them all").

Ken Crossen was married four times. With his first wife he had three children (Stephen, Karen, Kendra) and with his second a son (David). He lived in New York, Florida, Southern California, Nevada, and other parts of the country. Milo March moves from Denver to New York City after five books of the series, with an apartment on Perry Street in Greenwich Village; that's where Ken lived, too. His and Milo's favorite watering hole was the Blue Mill Tavern, a short walk from the apartment.

Ken Crossen was a combination of many of the traits of his different male characters: tough, adventuresome, with a taste for gin and shapely women. But perhaps the best observation was made in an obituary written by sci-fi writer Avram Davidson, who described Ken as a fundamentally gentle person who had been buffeted by many winds.